"I didn't have a tree last year."

He peered down   need to go buy on

"I see. How   ed toward the c   de the bookcase

"I like that look."

His approval had her biting her lip. When did things get so easy between them? Like this was the way they were meant to be.

She quickly shook off the crazy notion.

Kenzie handed Matt a book. "Will you read this to me?"

"Sure." He took a seat on the couch. "Hop on up here."

Lacie watched as Kenzie snuggled against his broad chest. Definitely one of the sweetest things she'd seen in a long time.

It was obvious that Kenzie was growing attached to Matt, making Lacie feel bad about taking her away.

A job in Telluride would mean she and Kenzie could stay in Ouray. Though it would also mean spending a lot of time with Matt, fighting to keep her feelings in check.

And that was a risk Lacie wasn't sure she was willing to take.

It took **Mindy Obenhaus** forty years to figure out what she wanted to do when she grew up. But once God called her to write, she never looked back. She's passionate about touching readers with biblical truths in an entertaining, and sometimes adventurous, manner. Mindy lives in Texas with her husband and kids. When she's not writing, she enjoys cooking and spending time with her grandchildren. Find more at mindyobenhaus.com.

Books by Mindy Obenhaus

Love Inspired

Rocky Mountain Heroes
Their Ranch Reunion
The Deputy's Holiday Family

The Doctor's Family Reunion
Rescuing the Texan's Heart
A Father's Second Chance
Falling for the Hometown Hero

The Deputy's Holiday Family

Mindy Obenhaus

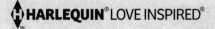

Recycling programs
for this product may
not exist in your area.

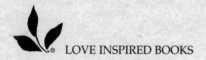 LOVE INSPIRED BOOKS

ISBN-13: 978-0-373-89973-9

The Deputy's Holiday Family

Copyright © 2017 by Melinda Obenhaus

www.Harlequin.com

Printed in U.S.A.

For all have sinned and fall short
of the glory of God, and all are justified
freely by His grace through the redemption
that came by Christ Jesus.
—*Romans* 3:23–24

To my loving husband, Richard.
You are my hero.

Acknowledgments

Many thanks to former Ouray County deputy
Betty Wolfe, and theater arts teacher
Alyssa Preston for all of your valuable input.
I couldn't have done this without you.

Chapter One

Coming home had never been so bittersweet.

Lacie Collier tapped her brakes at the Ouray city limit sign, observing the snowcapped mountains that closed in around her. Okay, so her trip home in February for her sister's funeral ranked right up there, too. But this was different.

She glimpsed the brown-eyed little girl in her rearview mirror. The last nine months had been quite an adjustment period for both her and Kenzie. And while her niece seemed to finally be adapting to life without her mother, Lacie was still struggling to balance motherhood and work. Or was anyway, until her employer decided the addition of a child was too distracting and let Lacie go.

Her heart ached as she approached the hot springs pool. She'd wanted so badly to make this the best Christmas ever for Kenzie. Now they didn't even have a home.

Still, God had a plan, of that she was certain. She just wished He'd give her some clue as to what lay ahead.

"Are we there yet?" Poor Kenzie. They'd spent the last five-plus hours driving across Colorado. A trip Lacie never relished, but throw a four-year-old into the mix and it became an even greater challenge.

"Almost, sweetie. We'll be at Grandma's in just a few more minutes." She knew the kid was eager to break free of the booster seat that held her captive.

Past the park, Main Street greeted them with all of its intimate charm. To the unsuspecting traveler, Ouray was simply a slowdown on their journey along Highway 550, but to those who had taken the time to stop, it was a treasure trove of everything from arts to adventure, four-wheeling to hiking, ice climbing to hot springs.

She slowed the car to almost a crawl, taking in the Victorian-era buildings and the sidewalks bustling with activity. Though it was only the Saturday before Thanksgiving, the town was already decked out for Christmas. Giant lighted snowflakes and evergreen garlands adorned every light post, stores sparkled with holiday-themed window displays, and twinkling lights were everywhere you looked. Everywhere except Barbara Collier's house. Because her mom didn't do Christmas.

She let go a frustrated sigh. How was she ever going to make this Christmas special for Kenzie?

A squeal erupted from the back seat.

Lacie's gaze instantly jerked to her niece and the toy-filled back seat. "What's wrong?"

"My drink," Kenzie whined, her light-up shoes flickering with each and every kick of her suddenly wet legging-clad legs.

"Oh, no." Lacie grabbed the wad of fast-food napkins from the passenger seat. "Did you spill?" With one hand still on the steering wheel, she tried in vain to blot the little girl's legs.

Kenzie merely nodded, her bottom lip pooched out.

Still attempting to console the child, Lacie glanced at the road in front of her, sympathy instantaneously morphing into horror as a pedestrian dodged out of her way.

With a loud gasp, she slammed on the brakes, her seat belt tightening in protest.

Kenzie cried in earnest now as Lacie put the vehicle into Park and fumbled to release her restraint. Her heart thudding, she pushed her door open, the cold air slapping her in the face as she rushed toward the gray-haired woman. "I am so sorry. Are you okay?"

"I'm fine, young lady." Aged green eyes narrowed on her. "But you need to watch where you're going."

"I know. I apologize."

"And you also need to think about moving your car." The woman pointed.

Lacie turned to see a line of vehicles behind her. Not to mention all the people who'd gathered at the corner to see what was happening.

"Yes, ma'am." She hurried back to her SUV, praying nobody recognized her. Then, with Kenzie's whimpers still echoing from the back seat, Lacie double-checked for pedestrians and continued up the street. *Thank You, God, that I didn't hit that woman.*

Half a block later, she heard the whine of a siren. She eyed her mirrors to discover flashing lights bearing down on her. "Perfect."

With not a parking spot to be had on Main Street, she turned at the next corner and eased into the first available space.

"Are we there?" Hope laced Kenzie's voice.

"Sorry, sweetie." She again put the vehicle into Park, gathered her courage, along with her license, registration and proof of insurance, and drew in a shaky breath before rolling down her window. This day couldn't possibly get any worse.

Shielding her eyes from the sun, she watched as the deputy exited his Tahoe and started toward her. Somewhere around six foot and well-built, he wore a black ball cap embroidered with a gold sheriff's badge over his short dark hair, but sunglasses made it impossible to see his eyes. A tactical vest with a plethora of pockets covered his tan shirt and she caught the name on his badge as the sunglasses came off.

Stephens.

One look at his dark gaze and her insides cringed. Obviously, she was wrong, because things had just gotten worse.

Out of the five Stephens brothers, why did it have to be Matt? The one who'd been her good friend through most of high school and the one she'd secretly crushed on…until he started dating her sister.

She sank lower into her seat. Their friendship was never the same after that.

"I thought that was you, Lacie."

She had to force herself to look at him, though when she did, his smile made it impossible to turn away. "Yep, it's me, all right." How could it be that he was even more handsome than she remembered when he hadn't really changed at all, save for the slight creases around his almond-shaped eyes. And those lips with that perfect Cupid's bow—

Whoa! Wrong train of thought for Matt Stephens or any other guy. While Marissa may have thought it fine to have a bunch of men traipsing in and out of her life, Lacie wanted better for Kenzie. She deserved security, a good home and a happy life. Which was why Lacie had to find another job and get back to Denver as soon as possible.

Matt rested a forearm against the roof of her vehicle and glanced toward the back seat. "You doin' okay? Looked like you were having a little problem back there on Main Street."

"Yeah." She brushed a wayward hair away from her face. "I got distracted, that's all."

"That's *all*?" He straightened then, crossing his arms over his chest. "You almost took out Mrs. Wells."

"I know." Her shoulders sagged. "I'm sorry. My niece was having a problem and I—"

"Could have killed somebody."

Was he deliberately trying to make her feel worse?

"Lacie, you know you're supposed to stop for pedestrians in the crosswalk."

"Yes, yes, I do. And it won't happen again. I promise."

"I'm sure it won't." His breath puffed in the cold afternoon air. "But I'm afraid I'm still going to have to give you ticket."

Indignation had her sitting taller. "A ticket? Why? Nobody got hurt."

"I'm sorry, Lacie, but you broke the law."

"It wasn't like I did it on purpose."

"Nobody ever plans to have an accident." He pulled a pad from his vest. "I'll need to see your license, registration and proof of—"

"Yeah, yeah." She shoved the documents toward him.

"You know, you could cut me a little slack. I'm just doing my job."

She forced herself to smile. "Or you could cut me some and let me off with a warning."

Chuckling, he patted her on the arm. "I'll be right back."

She could hardly wait.

"Aunt Lacie?"

"What is it, sweetie?" Turning, she noticed that not only was Kenzie no longer crying, but her deep brown eyes were as wide as she'd ever seen them.

"Are we going to go to jail?"

She couldn't help smiling. "No, we are not going to jail. As soon as we're done here, we're going straight to Grandma's to get you cleaned up and into some dry clothes. Okay?"

The little girl grinned. "Okay."

"All right. Here you go, Lacie."

She twisted back toward the door to accept her documents from Matt.

"And if I could just get you to sign here." Pointing with his pen, he handed her his ticket pad. "You two in for Thanksgiving?"

And then some, but he didn't need to know that.

"We are, yeah." She scrawled her name. Why did he make her so nervous? After all, it wasn't like they were in high school anymore. She was thirty-four years old, for crying out loud.

Must be the uniform.

She handed him his pad.

Or the fact that he's every bit as good-looking as you remembered.

He tore off her copy then bent to hand it to her, his seemingly curious gaze drifting from her to Kenzie. "Be safe and I hope you guys have a happy Thanksgiving." With a wink, he walked away.

She looked at the ticket in her hand. So much for old friends.

No telling how much it was going to cost her for almost killing someone. Yet as she continued to study the paper, she suddenly found herself smiling.

It wasn't a ticket at all. He *had* given her a warning.

* * *

Matt couldn't seem to get Lacie out of his mind. And, for the life of him, he couldn't figure out why. Nonetheless, he'd spent the last twenty-four hours thinking of little else.

Was it the frazzled state she seemed to be in? Or the way she'd glared at him with those pretty gray-blue eyes?

Perhaps it was the little girl in the back seat. Though he may have been much older, he knew the pain of losing a mother. And with no father in the picture, Marissa's death had likely rocked the kid's world.

Memories of the child's mother played across his mind. The last time he'd seen Marissa was six years ago, when he was stationed in Hawaii with the navy. Her visit had been a pleasant surprise. And for a brief time, he'd even thought their failed relationship might have a second chance. Instead, he'd gotten burned, and discovered the kind of person Marissa had really been. Evidently the old adage was true. Beauty is only skin-deep.

He scrubbed a hand over his face. The Collier women were the last thing he should be dwelling on. Not when he had plenty of other things to worry about. Like work, his father and the town's annual Christmas play. He could only imagine what Dad would think of him taking on the role of director.

Something Matt wasn't 100 percent sure of himself. He was just a deputy sheriff who barely knew stage right from stage left. Yet when he heard rumors that they were thinking about canceling the play, he'd felt compelled to do something. He couldn't let the event his mother had begun over a decade ago die. That would be like losing Mama all over again.

So here he sat in the cab of his Jeep, staring at the two-story cream-and-blue brick building that was the Wright Opera House, praying he wouldn't let her down.

Drawing in a deep breath, he grabbed the stack of scripts from the passenger seat and stepped out into the chilly late-afternoon air. The cast would be arriving soon, so he'd better get inside and at least pretend he knew what he was doing. He refused to let other people see him as the screwup his father believed him to be. Because regardless of the what the old man thought, Matt was not responsible for his mother's death.

He flipped on the lights inside the circa 1888 building that smelled of lemon oil and popcorn. Moving past the box office with its intricately carved moldings, he continued up the curved staircase to the second floor. The view at the top never ceased to stop him in his tracks.

Beyond the expanse of arched windows, the gray volcanic peaks of the Amphitheater enveloped the town's eastern edge. Cloaked in white and skirted with conifers, they were a sight to behold. God's majesty on full display.

A few steps closer and his gaze fell to a nearly empty Main Street. He could only imagine how things must have looked back when Ouray was a thriving mining town. Carriages lining Main Street as people turned out in their finest for some cultural enrichment.

With an about-face, he moved into the theater opposite the windows and brought up the house lights. Unexpected emotion clogged his throat as he took in the large space with its brick walls, wooden floor and the original stage curtain that now served as a mural. Mama used to think of the Wright as her second home. He could still see her, taking the stage in an array of roles—everything from a soldier to a nun. She may have been a country girl, but she loved the theater. And this play was her legacy. Meaning as long as Matt lived and breathed, the show would go on.

"Oh, good. I'm not the first one here."

The voice had him whirling to find Lacie

standing behind him. Her caramel-colored hair, which had been pulled back into a ponytail yesterday, now spilled over her shoulders and down her back. Much longer than the no-nonsense, chin-length style she'd worn throughout high school. And with her pale pink peacoat cinched around her waist, she was quite the contrast to the tomboy who had once run circles around him and just about every other guy on the basketball court at Ouray High. She'd always steered clear of anything remotely feminine. That is, until she took the stage their senior year. Watching her transform from the Cockney Eliza Doolittle into a refined lady in their school play had had everyone's jaw dropping.

Her smile wavered as he approached, her expression suddenly curious. "What are you doing here?"

He cleared his throat. "I'm directing the Christmas play. Why are you here?"

"I'm *in* the play." Hands stuffed inside the pockets of her coat, she shifted from one stylishly booted foot to the other. "I thought Mrs. Nichols was directing. That's what she said when she called and invited me to be a part of it."

"You're only in town for Thanksgiving. Why would she ask you to be in the play?"

Lacie hesitated a moment before jutting her chin out. "Actually... I'm here throughout WinterFest."

But that ran from Thanksgiving all the way to the ice festival in January, so— "Why would you do that?"

A hint of annoyance pinched her brow. "Not that it's any of your business, but my mom needed some holiday help at the boutique." Removing her hands from her pockets, she brushed something from her coat sleeve. "And since I no longer have a job..."

She'd lost her job? Now he was really glad he'd given her only a warning. After all, she had a child to care for. "I'm sorry to hear that."

"It's only temporary." She looked everywhere but at him, seemingly studying everything from ceiling to floor. "So where's Mrs. Nichols?"

"Rehab."

Eyes wide, she finally met his gaze.

"She broke her hip."

"Ooh, that's rough. She's such a sweet woman."

"Yes, she is."

Lacie meandered toward the windows. "Great theater teacher, too. I hope she recovers soon."

"We all do."

After a silent moment, she faced him. "So you're directing the play in her stead?"

"Yes, I am."

"I…didn't realize you were into theater."

"I'm not. But my mother was. The Christmas play was her baby." He lifted a shoulder. "And since there was no one else willing to direct…"

A hint of a smile played across her pink lips. "That's actually very sweet. I know how close you were to your mother."

Sentiment prevented him from responding with anything but a nod.

"That reminds me, though," she continued. "I wanted to thank you."

"For what?"

"For giving me a warning instead of a ticket." Hands back in her pockets, she shrugged. "In case you couldn't tell, I was kind of freaked out about what had happened. That warning made my day a little bit better."

Something about that last statement warmed him. "Glad I could help."

"So where is everyone else?" She looked to the street as an echo of voices drifted from downstairs.

"Sounds like they just arrived."

A short time later, after moving a few rows of chairs out of the way, he gathered in front of the stage with the dozen or so cast members comprised of townsfolk ranging in age from eighteen to seventy.

"I want to thank you all for coming and for

being a part of this play." He filled them in on Mrs. Nichols's condition. "Now, I know many of you have been involved in this event for many years. However, I'm new to this directing thing, so if any of you would like to bow out, this would be your chance."

"Don't be silly, Matt." Valerie Dawson waved off his comment. She'd been a good friend of his mother's and a part of this event since its inception. "We're just happy you were willing to step in on such short notice. Besides, it'll be nice to have a Stephens leading us again."

A round of nods and "that's rights" followed, bolstering his confidence. Maybe this wouldn't be so hard, after all.

"All right, then. Since this is supposed to be a read-through, I guess I'll just pass out these scripts—" he picked up the stack from the edge of the stage "—and we'll get started."

"Excuse me." Lacie held up her hand. "Are we not going to go over show expectations?"

Show expectations? What were those?

"Do you have our call times?" asked someone else.

Call times? Okay, that was rehearsals. At least he thought that's what they were.

"Oh, and what about costumes?" asked another. "When will we be fitted?"

Matt wasn't used to having his authority

questioned. Then again, he wasn't wearing a uniform, either. He was completely out of his element.

He scanned the expectant faces before him, not wanting to let them down. Yet there was one glaring factor he couldn't ignore.

He was in *way* over his head. Having Lacie here only amplified his incompetence. And he got the feeling she didn't like him much, either. Two things he was determined to change.

Chapter Two

He was crashing and burning. And Lacie couldn't bear to watch. Not after hearing why he'd chosen to become their director. She had to help him out.

Suddenly nervous, though, she hesitated, glancing at the faces around her. While she knew most of the people, one she even used to babysit, she'd been gone from Ouray for a long time. She didn't want to come across as a know-it-all, no matter how much community theater she'd done. A cast was a team, no one person better than another. She supposed she should have remembered that when she brought up the show expectations.

Still, she had to do something.

With lights glaring overhead, she raised her hand again and mustered her most charming smile. "You know what? I think we're all eager to do the read-through, so let's not worry about the technicalities right now."

"You are absolutely right, Lacie," said Valerie. "Let's get on with the read-through."

"No, no." Matt set the scripts back down on the edge of the stage. "If the show expectations come first, then we will cover them now."

What? It was obvious he didn't have a clue what show expectations were. And yet when she'd given him an out, he ignored it.

Let him fail then.

No, that wasn't right or Christian of her. Though it was apparent he didn't want anyone to interfere.

Hands slung low on his denim-clad hips, he continued, "I want to do this right. So let's go ahead and discuss our expectations." He scanned the group before him. "Rehearsal times are firm. In case you aren't aware, I'm former military, which means I'm a stickler for promptness."

The cast was silent, giving him their full attention. The military reference must have scared them.

The corners of his mouth lifted a notch. "However, I'm also a realist. As a law enforcement officer, I know how life can interfere. Before you leave tonight, I will give each of you my cell number. If you're going to be late, please let me know."

She had to give him credit for trying.

"Now that we've got that out of the way—" he reached for the scripts "—let's continue with the read-through."

One by one he passed out the scripts, though she was beginning to wish she hadn't signed on for this. No matter how much she loved acting, she'd agreed to work with Mrs. Nichols, not Matt Stephens, the man who didn't have a clue he'd broken her heart.

"*The Bishop's Wife*." His baritone voice carried throughout the space. "Mr. Garcia, would you get us started, please?"

For the next hour and a half, Lacie focused on the script as well as the rest of the cast instead of the man leading them. And once they were finished, she was eager to leave. After chatting with Clare Droste, the girl she'd once babysat, Lacie donned her coat and started across the wooden floor. Maybe she'd even make it back to her mother's in time for dinner.

"Lacie?"

Her steps slowed. Matt's voice set her nerves on edge.

Hands in her pockets, she turned on her heel. "Yes?"

He took a step closer. "Would you mind staying? I'd like to talk with you."

Talk with or talk to? She had questioned him, after all.

Reluctantly, she made her way through the cluster of exiting cast members, toward the stage and the man she'd seen more of in the past two days than she had in the past sixteen years.

"Was there something you needed?"

"Yes." Hands clasped, he leaned against the edge of the stage. "How much acting have you done?"

She crossed her arms over her chest. "Until Kenzie came to live with me, quite a bit."

"I suspected as much."

"Is that a problem?"

"No. It's just that—" he pushed away from the stage "—well, I have no idea what I'm doing here. I was wondering if you'd be willing to teach me?"

Her arms fell to her sides. "Teach you?"

"Yes."

"Teach you what? Acting?"

"What I'm supposed to be doing as a director."

"Oh. You mean you really don't know?"

He shook his head. "All I ever did was help with the set crew. And even that was only for a couple of years before Mama got sick."

Why did he have to keep bringing up his mother? Just thinking about Mona made it much more difficult to say no. And she wanted to say no. Just the thought of being with Matt made her edgy. "If you could just walk me through some of the terminology and what I need to do at each step in the process."

"I really should be getting home to Kenzie." She poked a thumb toward the exit.

"It doesn't have to be tonight. The group doesn't meet again until next Sunday."

"Yes, and there's Thanksgiving and—"

"Please?" His velvet brown eyes pleaded with her. "I don't want to mess this up, Lacie."

She did not want to be around Matt Stephens any more than necessary. Unfortunately, a successful play fell into the "necessary" category. The entire town looked forward to this event.

"Okay, I'll help." Letting go a sigh, she pulled her phone from her pocket. "What's your email address?"

"Email?"

"Yes, so I can send you a list of things you need to do."

"Okay. But can we meet at least once to go over it?"

She'd rather have a root canal. They gave you painkillers for that. "Fine. But I hope you don't mind kids, because Kenzie will likely be accompanying me."

"Not a problem. We can even meet at your mother's, if you like."

She typed in the email address he gave her. "I'll send you something later tonight or tomorrow morning. Then we can schedule a meeting." Tucking her phone back into her pocket, she continued. "Right now, I need to get home to my niece."

Outside, she tightened the belt on her peacoat and shivered. Seemed the temperatures had gone down along with the sun. It was downright freezing.

She hurried across the darkened street to her SUV, wishing she'd brought her gloves. She'd forgotten how much colder it could be here than in Denver. Of course, Ouray was also more than two thousand feet higher in altitude.

Under the glow of a street lamp, she threw herself into the driver's seat, shoved the key into the ignition and gave it a twist. Except instead of the engine roaring to life, it simply clicked. Weird. She turned the key again. *Weeneeneeneenee... Weeneenee, weeneenee...*

She groaned, recalling the words of the mechanic who'd done her last oil change.

"You're probably going to want to think about changing out that battery soon."

And she'd just driven all the way across the state.

Stupid! How could she have let that slip?

As the windows started to fog, she willed herself to calm down. All she needed was someone to give her a jump.

She opened her door and stepped out onto Ouray's only paved street, looking around for anyone who might be able to help her. But with the other cast members long gone, things were pretty deserted.

A gust of wind sent her back inside her vehicle. "Lord, please help me to get this started."

Once again, she twisted the key and was met with the same result.

Tap, tap, tap.

She jumped, jerking her head toward the window.

"Need a little help?" Matt stood on the other side, wearing a smile that would melt most women's hearts. But she wasn't most women.

She pushed the door open. "My battery could use a jump."

"Sure. Just let me swing my Jeep over here."

"I've got jumper cables," she called after him. No point in having him think she was incapable of taking care of herself.

In no time, his vehicle was nose-to-nose with hers, cables extending between them, and she was back behind the wheel, praying her car would start.

"All right, Lacie," he hollered from outside. "Give it a try."

With a nod, she turned the key.

Weenee...

"No, please don't do this to me."

"One more time." He sent her a thumbs-up.

Please, please, please... She tried again.

Nothing. Not one sound.

Matt opened her door then. "I'm afraid your battery is dead."

She wanted to cry. Though not in front of him.

So she grabbed her purse and keys and stepped outside. "I guess I'll just have to walk home."

"No, I'll give you a ride."

She dared to look at him now. "It's not that far. I'll be perfectly—"

"You're just as stubborn as ever, aren't you, Lacie?"

She froze. Lace? He was the only one who'd ever called her that. Something just between them, an endearment that made her feel...special.

"Well, so am I," he continued. "And I am not about to let you walk. So get in the Jeep while I take care of these cables."

She simply stared at him, though she wasn't sure what bugged her most. The fact that he called her stubborn or that he thought he could tell her what to do. However, since her teeth were chattering and her fingers and toes were numb, she climbed into the passenger seat and waited.

He tossed the cables into the back before getting in the driver's seat. "All right, let's get you home."

Couldn't come soon enough for her. Being around Matt was so…nerve-racking.

He put the vehicle into gear and turned at the corner. "So are you hoping to find a job closer to Ouray?"

"Oh, no." Looking out the window, she watched the houses go by. "Denver is our home. Kenzie has her daycare, our friends are there, our church… I don't want to uproot her. I'm just biding my time until I have something else lined up." Unfortunately, none of the home builders in the Denver area were looking to hire anyone, including interior designers/stagers until after the holidays.

"That's very commendable." He turned onto her mother's street. "A shame, too."

"Why?"

"I'm sure your mother would enjoy having both you and your niece near."

"Oh." She tamped down the unwanted disappointment. "Well, I just want what's best for

Kenzie." Not to mention herself. And that meant keeping her heart closed to Matt Stephens.

She reached for the door handle as he eased to a stop in front of Mom's house. "Thanks for the ride."

Gray clouds and freezing temperatures were the order of the day as Matt climbed the front steps at the Collier house shortly before nine the next morning. When he'd dropped Lacie off last night, he'd barely brought his Jeep to a stop before she hopped out. Leaving him to wonder why she was being so standoffish.

Sure they hadn't seen each other in years, but time couldn't erase the fact that they'd once been really good friends. From seventh to eleventh grade, they'd had no problem confiding in one another. Then he'd started dating Marissa and Lacie no longer wanted anything to do with him. Just like last night.

Later Marissa told him Lacie had had a crush on him. Making him feel like the biggest jerk ever for not recognizing it.

But that was sixteen years ago. That couldn't be the problem now, could it?

Regardless, his friend had a dead battery to contend with and her mother had a business to run. Even if Lacie were to use Barbara's car, she'd still have to remove the battery and find a replacement all with a child in tow. He couldn't let her do that. Not in this weather.

He knocked on the door of the slate-colored, sixties-era, single-story rambler, thinking of all the times he'd been there before. Back when two teenage girls lived there and the house was an ugly pea green. Much had changed in the last sixteen years. And not all for the better.

The door swung open then and Barbara Collier smiled at him, just as she had all those years ago. These days, her short, dark blond hair sported a little more gray and her blue eyes had lost some of their spark, but given what she'd been through, having lost her husband and a daughter, he supposed it was understandable.

She pushed open the storm door. "Matt, what a pleasant surprise." Her gaze skimmed his uniform. "At least, I hope so." She looked him in the eye again. "You're not here on official business, are you?"

He couldn't help chuckling. "No, ma'am. You're in the clear."

"Well, in that case, come on in."

He wiped his booted feet on the mat before following her inside the comfortable living room with its pale yellow walls and overstuffed beige furniture.

"Can I get you some coffee?" She gestured to the adjoining kitchen.

"No, thank you. I don't suppose Lacie's up, is sh—"

"I'm gonna get you, you little stinker." Lacie's voice trailed down the hallway to the right, as a small child came running into the room wearing bright pink pajamas.

"No…" The little girl laughed and bounded onto the couch.

"I've got you now." Lacie closed in on her, stopping short when she spotted Matt. "I didn't know we had company."

"Don't let me interrupt your fun," he said with a smile.

She grabbed the small shirt and pants that were draped over her shoulder. "Somebody's giving me a hard time about getting dressed this morning."

The child grew quiet and clung to her aunt's leg once she realized there was a stranger in the house. She was a cute little thing. Dark brown curls, dark eyes… Not at all like Marissa. Yet there was something about her.

Obviously sensing the girl's hesitation, Barbara said, "Kenzie, this is our friend Officer Matt."

Did she remember him from the other day, when he'd pulled Lacie over?

Moving closer, he felt almost mesmerized as

he crouched to her level. She was little, all right. How old was she anyway? Three? Maybe four?

"It's nice to meet you, Kenzie."

Her smile returned, albeit a shy one as she tightened her hold on Lacie. Still, the pleasure it brought him was inexplicable. Never had a stranger's eyes looked so familiar.

"What brings you by?" Lacie's tone carried that same stubborn edge he'd heard yesterday.

"You."

Her eyes widened as he stood. "Me?"

"Yes. You have a dead battery that needs to be replaced. I'm here to help."

"Oh, that won't be—"

"That is so sweet of you, Matt." Barbara made her way toward them. "Lacie's been stressing all morning, wondering if she was going to need to have her car towed or not."

One glance at a chagrined Lacie had him biting back a smile. "Nope, no towing needed. We'll simply take out the old battery, pick up a new one and put it in right there on Main Street."

"We?" Lacie's glare bounced between him and her mother.

"Okay, you'll just be there to supervise and pay for the battery. I'll do the rest."

She looked over his uniform. "But you're

working. I'm sure you have plenty of deputy things to keep you busy."

"Helping the community *is* part of my work."

She paused. "Well, what about Kenzie? I can't let her ride in the back seat of a sheriff's vehicle."

Man, she really did not want his help. Or was simply too obstinate to accept it.

"That's all right, dear," said Barbara. "Kenzie can come to the shop with me." She smiled at her granddaughter. "You want to come to work with Grandma?"

"Uh-huh."

"Okay, we'll have to get you dressed first." Barbara snagged the clothes from Lacie, then held out her other hand to Kenzie, who promptly took hold and accompanied her grandmother down the hall.

He managed to contain the laughter bubbling inside him. "Looks like we're free to go whenever you're ready."

Lacie continued to stare down the hall. While he'd appreciated her mother's intervention, it was obvious Lacie didn't share his opinion. "I'll get my coat."

"Might want to grab some gloves, too. It's kind of cold out there." After last night, he figured a friendly reminder wouldn't hurt.

Though, based on the look she sent him, she found his suggestion more irritating than friendly.

A short time later, he pulled behind her SUV on a slowly awakening Main Street.

"You can wait here, if you like. I just need to remove the old battery and—"

Lacie unhooked her seat belt. "I want you to show me how to do it."

He glanced across the center console to her lined jacket. Definitely more work appropriate than that pink coat she'd worn yesterday. "That's admirable. Most women leave this sort of stuff to someone else."

"Yeah, well, maybe I'm not most women. Should I ever find myself in this situation again—"

"Hopefully you won't, but I understand. Why don't you go pop the hood while I grab a couple of tools?"

He watched the set of her shoulders and the determination in her stride as she walked toward her vehicle. He had no doubt that Lacie could do anything she set her mind to, whether it was acting, becoming an instant mother or auto repair.

"First thing we need to do is remove the cables from the battery." A semi rumbled past as he hovered over the frozen engine. "A wrench is better, but you could also use pliers."

"Okay." The expectant look on her face was beyond endearing.

He continued, explaining each step until the battery was freed. "All we have to do now is lift it out, go get a new one and we're golden."

"Golden," she said with a rapt smile on her face. "Where do we find a new one?"

"At the service station north of town. That is, assuming they have one in stock."

"And if they don't?" Worry creased her pretty brow.

"You pick it up tomorrow. No big deal."

Fortunately, they had one in stock. And when they returned to her SUV, Lacie insisted on carrying it. No small feat, since it weighed almost forty pounds. About the size of a small child. Though he doubted Kenzie weighed that much.

He shook his head. He couldn't seem to stop thinking about the kid. Her dark eyes had grabbed hold of him and refused to let go.

"All right, Lace, this is your chance."

"Chance for what?"

Strange. Until now, he never realized how much he'd missed that smile. The one that hinted at the tender heart behind the tough facade. The one that never failed to draw him in. "You get to install the battery."

Still hunched over with the weight of her load, she said, "Seriously?"

"I'm only here for assistance."

Her eyes sparkled. "Cool!"

Her attempts to lift the battery to the proper height failed immediately, though. She flared her nostrils. "Grrr..."

"Easy." He moved to the back seat and grabbed Kenzie's car seat. Setting it on the asphalt, he said, "Try standing on this."

She did, and it was just the boost she needed to set the battery into place.

"All right, Lace, what's next?"

"I don't know." A moment of panic flitted across her face. "The negative cable?"

"That's right." He handed her the wrench.

She cinched it into place, then connected the positive. "Screwdriver," she said, moving the bracket into position.

Finished, she handed him his tools, her gaze expectant.

"Go fire it up and let's see what we've got."

She hurried behind the wheel and a moment later the engine roared to life. "I did it!" She hopped out onto the pavement, thrusting a fist into the air. "Yes!"

This time he did laugh. He'd never seen someone get so excited over a battery.

Suddenly more subdued, she moved toward him, her expression softening. "Thank you for teaching me." The pink tinge of her cheeks grew deeper, heightening his awareness of just how pretty she was. Why hadn't he noticed that before? "I really appreciate it."

"And I appreciate your willingness to help me understand my job as director. It's important to me."

Peering up at him through long lashes, she said, "I know it is." Her gray-blue eyes held his for a moment, allowing him the slightest glimpse of the Lacie he'd once shared his secrets with. Then she stepped away to close the hood. "That reminds me, I still need to send you that list."

"That's okay. You had other things to worry about."

She nodded. "Well, I…guess I'd better go get Kenzie. We need to run to Montrose to pick up a birthday cake."

"Looks like we got this taken care of just in time then. Whose birthday?"

"Kenzie's." Her smile was like any proud mother's. "I can't believe she's five already."

"Five?" He took a step back. "But she's so small. I would have thought she was younger."

"Nope." She glanced up and down the street, as though unable to look at him. "So I should go."

"Yeah, of course." He gathered up his tools and placed them in the back of his vehicle as she drove away. What was wrong with him?

This nagging sensation that twisted through him hadn't been there before. Was it Lacie's appreciation getting to him? Or something more?

The negotiation had been rougher than Kathy indicated might be the case. "Well, I guess I was just putting some of my worries into

Chapter Three

Lacie pulled into a parking spot in front of her mother's shop, mentally chastising herself. In all her gratitude, she'd almost let her guard down with Matt. Something she couldn't afford to do with any man. She owed it to her niece to be that one constant in her life, instead of allowing herself to be distracted the way Marissa so often had.

Like the night her boyfriend crashed his car, robbing Kenzie of her mother and forever changing her life.

Still, Lacie appreciated Matt's willingness to guide her through the process of installing her new battery. Not dismissing her or trying to take over the way Brandon would have. In the two years they'd dated, Brandon had insisted on doing everything for her. At first, she thought he was just being chivalrous, but later realized

Mr. Know-It-All had a deep-seated need to feel superior to anyone and everyone. Including her.

Shaking off the unwanted thoughts, she exited her vehicle into the cold late-morning air. Judging by the gray clouds obscuring the tops of the mountains along the town's western edge, they'd soon be in for some snow. Kenzie would love that. Good thing Lacie had scooped up a couple of coats and some snow pants on clearance for her back in the spring when she still had a job. She didn't want to have to tap into her savings any more than necessary.

Turning, she glimpsed the beginnings of her mother's window display at The Paisley Elk, a little clothing boutique that catered mostly to women. So far, it consisted of batting "snow" and white lights, but then the contest for best Christmas display didn't start in earnest until next week, so there was likely plenty more to come.

Inside was another story, though. Lacie had to hand it to her mother. The boutique was definitely festive. Standing under a ceiling adorned with hundreds of twinkling LED lights, she realized just how adept her mother had become at feigning Christmas. Not a Christmas tree in sight. No nativity of any kind. Not even a hint of the traditional red and green, save for the occasional evergreen bough. No, this was commercialism at its best. And if there wasn't a prize involved—even if it wasn't anything more than bragging rights—she doubted Mom would do any decorations at all.

Still, The Paisley Elk had an undeniable appeal that would draw people in. Like the glistening purple and silver balls that appeared to float in midair just below the lights, adding a touch of color to the overhead charm. And, of course, everything was perfectly merchandised for maximum effect, with pops of glitz and glam everywhere you looked.

Now if Lacie could just convince her mother to decorate the house…

December 23 would mark twelve years since Lacie's father's death. She'd never forget coming home from the hospital and watching her mother take down every decoration in the house. They hadn't even opened their presents. Mom said she'd never celebrate Christmas again. And, so far, she'd held true to her word.

However, this was Kenzie's first Christmas without Marissa. They owed it to her to make it the best Christmas the kid could possibly have. That meant having a tree, presents and everything else Lacie and Marissa had enjoyed as kids.

"There you are." Mom draped a glittering silver pashmina scarf around the neck of a dress form sporting a pine-bough skirt adorned with silver ribbon, purple and silver balls, and peacock feathers. "How's the car?"

"Up and running again, I'm happy to say." She spotted Kenzie off to one side playing with— "Mom, is that Marissa's and my old dollhouse?"

"Sure is. I thought, since Kenzie will be here with us a lot and that old thing was just collecting dust in the basement, she might enjoy playing with it." Moving beside Lacie, she lowered her voice. "And I was right. She's been playing with it this entire time."

Lacie's heart grew hopeful. Perhaps Mom hadn't lost all sentiment.

She crossed to the small table where Kenzie was carefully moving the tiny furniture pieces, her smile widening with each step. The kid must have been having fun because she hadn't even noticed that Lacie was there.

Kneeling beside her niece, she said, "What are you doing?"

"Playing house." Tongue peeking out the corner of her mouth, Kenzie placed the miniature baby into the tiny crib.

"Are you having fun?"

Kenzie nodded, her expression somewhere between determined and delighted.

"I know just how you feel, Kenzikins." Lacie's father had built the dollhouse when she and Marissa were little. Like Kenzie, Lacie would spend hours rearranging furniture and contemplating different wall colors. No wonder she'd gone into interior design.

"Would you mind helping me assemble these, dear?" At the counter beside the cash register, Mom shoved glitter-covered branches into one of five tall galvanized buckets.

"Sure." She shrugged out of her coat, setting it beside the dollhouse before joining her mother.

Reaching for a trio of sparkling white branches, she mustered the courage to broach the topic of the holidays. "I noticed there wasn't a turkey in the fridge or freezer. Would you like me to pick one up?" One at a time, she plunged the stems into the Epsom salt snow.

"That won't be necessary." After admiring her handiwork, Mom picked up a spool of wide purple ribbon and stretched a length around the first bucket. "I thought we'd just go to Bon Ton or The Outlaw. No point in spending our day off in the kitchen when for all intents and purposes, Thanksgiving is just another day."

Had Mom's heart really grown that hard?

"No, it's not." She stared at the woman in disbelief. "Thanksgiving is when family and friends come together to give thanks for their blessings." *Like we used to do when Daddy was alive.*

Her mother smiled, seemingly unaffected by Lacie's comments. "Okay, you pick where we should eat then."

Passing the first bucket off to Mom for ribbon, Lacie reached for another cluster of branches. "Actually, I was kind of looking forward to some of your homemade dressing."

No response. Barbara Collier had always been good at avoiding conflict.

But Lacie wasn't willing to let it drop. "What if *I* cooked Thanksgiving dinner? Nothing fancy. Just some turkey, dressing—I'll need your recipe—and maybe a pumpkin pie. You wouldn't have to lift a finger."

"I don't know." Mom tied another swath of ribbon. "I hate for you to go to so much trouble."

"It's no trouble. I like to cook." Especially when she had people to cook for. "Throw in those traditional recipes and I'm a goner."

Mom was silent for a long moment. Finally, "Oh, all right. If you insist."

She wasn't aware she was insisting, but as long as they were on a roll… "And then, after dinner, maybe we could put up the Christmas tree." Biting her lip, she held her breath and stabbed another twig in the bucket.

But her mother remained focused on the task

at hand. Without so much as flinching, she said, "Lacie, you know I don't celebrate Christmas anymore. If you want to take Kenzie to some of the festivities around town, that's fine. But there is no Christmas at the house."

She glared at her mother. "There used to be."

How she used to love coming down the hallway Christmas morning to the glow of twinkling lights and the soft sound of Christmas carols playing in the background. So many memories. Memories she desperately wanted to recreate for Kenzie. *God, please soften Mom's heart.*

"That was a long time ago." Her mother moved her reading glasses to the top of her head and looked at Lacie. "People change."

"And you won't change for your granddaughter?"

Scooping up the two completed buckets, she whisked past Lacie to disperse them throughout the store. "We all have our beliefs and convictions. I have chosen not to celebrate Christmas."

The bell over the door jangled then, ushering in a customer and effectively ending their conversation. Even though Lacie had so much more to say.

She glimpsed the little girl across the room. No, that wasn't a discussion to be had while Kenzie was within earshot.

So she finished the other three buckets while Mom assisted her customer, then went to check on Kenzie. "Are you about ready to go pick out your birthday cake?"

The child beamed. "I want chocolate."

Turning her gaze to the window, Lacie couldn't help smiling. "Chocolate it is then."

Maybe she'd even get the kid to take a nap this afternoon, allowing Lacie to work on that list for Matt.

Thoughts of the deputy had her wondering what he was doing for Thanksgiving. Perhaps they should invite him to join them. As a thank-you for helping her today.

She rubbed her arms, quickly dismissing the ridiculous notion. He had his own family. A rather large one, at that.

Besides, she had better things to do than worry about Matt Stephens's Thanksgiving plans. Like figuring out how on earth she was going to have a Christmas for Kenzie when her mom was dead set against it.

An hour after Lacie pulled away, Matt sat at the counter at Granny's Kitchen, a local diner, staring at his untouched burger. Seemed no matter how hard he tried to erase the memory, his mind kept rewinding to one February night nearly six years ago. Marissa's last in Hawaii. A night that never should have happened.

His insides churned. The math added up. But still…

Marissa may have done him wrong, but she would have told him he had a child, wouldn't she? Then again, she hadn't told him she was dating someone else, either.

So why isn't Kenzie's dad raising her?

He picked up a fry and forced himself to take a bite. He didn't want to believe it. But he couldn't ignore it, either. Could Kenzie be his daughter?

"What's up with the sad face?" A hand clamped on to Matt's shoulder.

He looked up as his brother Andrew helped himself to one of his fries. "What are you doing here?"

Andrew plopped down in the seat beside him. "Carly's putting up the Christmas decorations at Granger House, so I'm on my own for lunch." For the past nineteen years, Andrew had lived in Denver, where he ran a multimillion-dollar commercial construction company. Until last spring when he sold it, came back to Ouray and married his high school sweetheart. Now they were stuck with him.

"Christmas decorations? It's not even Thanksgiving yet."

Andrew snagged another fry. "True, but we've got guests booked for this weekend, so the bed-and-breakfast portion of the house needs to be ready before then." His gaze drifted to Matt's plate. "Something wrong with your burger? You haven't touched it."

"Guess I'm not very hungry."

His cell buzzed in his pocket. He pulled it out to see Gladys Bricker's name on the screen. His favorite teacher must be baking again, because that was the only reason she ever called. A fiercely independent gal, Gladys had never married, but considered many of her former students her children. Himself included.

"Hello, Gladys."

"Oh, Matt, I hate to bother you."

Something in the eighty-one-year-old woman's voice wasn't quite right. "Gladys, you are never a bother. What can I do for you?"

"I'm afraid I need some wood brought in. It's already cut, but I just can't seem to make it outside to get it." His unease rose. That was definitely not like Gladys.

He stood. "Not to worry. I'm on my way." He ended the call. "Looks like your timing is perfect, bro." He slid his plate toward Andrew. "Duty calls."

His older brother reached for the burger. "I'll get the tab."

"You do that," said Matt as he made his way out the door into the brisk midday air. Honestly, he was grateful for Gladys's call. He wasn't exactly in the mood for a lengthy conversation with Andrew today. However, he was worried about the older woman.

He slid behind the wheel of his Tahoe and headed north, continuing outside of town. Gladys had always been faithful in keeping in touch with him over the years. He still had all the letters she'd sent him while he was in the navy.

A few minutes later, he pulled into her drive, gravel crunching beneath his tires. Exiting the vehicle, he spotted the large pile of wood near the barn at the back of the property. He made his way there first and filled his arms before heading to the small, white, single-story house with green trim.

He tugged open the screen door and knocked. "Gladys? It's Matt."

His anxiety heightened as the seconds dragged on. Reaching for the knob, he gave it a twist and inched the door open. "Gladys?"

"In—" coughing echoed from the living room that sat at the opposite end of the kitchen "—in here."

He continued into the house, moving through the compact yet tidy kitchen and into the chilly living room. There, on the other side of the room, in front of the big picture window, the elderly woman lay in her recliner, buried under a stack of blankets, her short gray hair sticking up every which way. She looked frailer than he'd ever imagined.

Crossing to the wood-burning stove in the corner of the room, he dropped the wood before touching a hand to the side of the stove. "This thing is stone-cold." He opened the door to see only ashes in the bottom.

He twisted around. "What's going on, Gladys? Why don't you have a fire going?"

Her face was pale, but she sent him weak smile. "I ran out of wood."

This wasn't good. "You're sick, aren't you?"

"Just a little cold." One wrinkled hand clasped the blankets to her chest while the other held tightly to a handkerchief she used to cover her mouth when she coughed.

A few quick strides put him at her side. He touched her forehead. "You're burning up."

"Am I?" Clouded blue eyes met his. "Feels pretty chilly to me."

He knelt beside her. "Have you been to see the doctor?"

"No."

He knew what he had to do, but Gladys wasn't going to like it. The best thing he could do was to make her a little more comfortable before bringing up the ambulance. A few more minutes wouldn't make that much difference.

"Okay, let me get this fire started." Back at the stove, he removed the ashes before adding a starter stick from the box he spotted on the shelf and a couple of thin logs.

After closing the doors, he went into the kitchen and set the four-cup coffeepot to brew. Probably not the best thing, but she needed something warm. A few minutes later, he filled an old green coffee cup halfway and took it to her. "Careful, it's hot."

"Thank you, Matt. You're a good boy."

No, a good boy would have checked on her more often.

After adding another log to the firebox, he pulled up a chair and sat beside her. "I wish you had called me earlier."

"I know. But I—"

"Hate to bother me, I know." Resting his forearms on his thighs, he leaned closer. "Gladys, I need to call an ambulance."

Her eyes widened slightly as she passed him her cup.

"I'm afraid you have more than just a cold and I want the EMTs to come and check you out."

"Can't I just go to the doctor?" She coughed.

"And how are you going to get there? You're

in no condition to drive yourself." Any other time he'd take her himself, but since he was the only deputy on duty... Besides, she'd likely be going to the hospital in Montrose anyway.

Her thin lips pursed as she turned her gaze to the conifer-dotted landscape outside the window. "If you think that would be best."

He laid a hand atop hers. "I do. I want you to get better."

He made the call, then monitored the fire and paced the beige carpet as he waited for the EMTs to arrive.

"When did you do this?" He pointed to two photos, one color, the other black-and-white, encased in a single frame on the wall near the opening to the kitchen.

"About a month ago. That's my first graduating class—" more coughing "—and my last graduating class." Forty years of teaching. Definitely impressive.

"Hey, there's me." He pointed to the newer photo.

"Bring it over here, please."

He lifted the frame and took it to her.

She smiled as she touched the glass. "You and your brothers all had your father's dark eyes."

"Except Daniel," he said. The baby of the family was the polar opposite with his blond hair and blue eyes.

"Oh, yes. He took after your mother. But the rest of you… Anyone could tell you were a Stephens."

His gut clenched, images of Kenzie flashing through his mind. Her dark eyes. That sense of familiarity washed over him again. Could it be true?

Thirty minutes after the EMTs arrived, he watched as they loaded Gladys into the back of the ambulance. While bronchitis was a good bet, given her age, the doctors wanted to observe her to be certain there was nothing else going on.

He returned to the house to make sure everything was in order and the fire in the wood stove was put out. He'd have to touch base with the church and others in town so Gladys would have plenty of folks to check on her and bring her food once she returned home.

Before leaving, he picked up the framed photo and hung it back on the wall. *Anyone could tell you were a Stephens.*

His eyes closed. *God, forgive me. I know I made a mistake all those years ago. How do I know if Kenzie is my child?*

By the time his shift ended, he could hardly wait to get home. He didn't want to get his hopes up, but if what played across his brain was truly from God, he might have the answer he'd prayed for.

He pulled his Tahoe into the drive, ditched his gear at the back door and headed straight for the bookshelves surrounding the fireplace in the living room. Quickly locating the scrapbook his mother had compiled for him and his sister-in-law Carly had assembled, he flipped past the baby pictures and those of him as a toddler, his heart pounding when he came to a photo of him at age four and a half. Except the face staring back at him was Kenzie's. The nose, the eyes— He touched a finger to his forehead—even that little widow's peak had Stephens written all over it.

He dropped onto the couch, feeling as though the air had been sucked from his lungs.

Kenzie was his daughter.

Chapter Four

Standing at the island in her mother's kitchen, Lacie transferred the remnants of Kenzie's birthday cake to a large plastic container then licked a smudge of the super sweet frosting from her finger. Thanks to no nap earlier in the day, save for fifteen short minutes in the car on the way back from Montrose, the little girl had crashed early. Still, it had been a good birthday. Mom had gone above and beyond on the gifts. Clothes, toys, books... Yet she refused to do Christmas. Unless the abundance was to make up for *not* celebrating Christmas.

Whatever the case, they'd all had a pleasant evening.

She stowed the cake in the fridge, rinsed and dried her hands, then grabbed her laptop and settled on the couch in the living room. Since she'd sent off Matt's list this afternoon, she was now free to see if any new job listings had been posted. Because if she could find something that started before Christmas, her problems would be solved.

"I see you got a turkey." Sitting in an adjacent chair near the window, Mom looked up from her book and moved her reading glasses to the top of her head.

Lacie lifted a brow. Was that merely an observation or were they about to enter round two of holiday discussions? If so, she'd better prepare to stand her ground.

"Just a small one." She snagged the deep purple plush throw from the back of the sofa and tossed it over her legs while she waited for the website to load. "Oh, and don't forget to give me your dressing recipe."

"It's in the recipe file in the cupboard." Mom reached for her herbal tea on the side table. "It's fairly basic, no special ingredients, so you shouldn't have any trouble finding what you need at Duckett's."

Contemplating an inevitable trip to Ouray's one and only grocer, Lacie was pleased to see that her mother had embraced the idea of having Thanksgiving here at the house. Now if she would just come around to Lacie's way of thinking regarding Christmas...

A knock sounded at the door.

She and her mother exchanged quizzical looks.

"I wonder who that could be." Mom set her cup down, stood and started for the door. Fingering the sheer curtain aside, she peered through the sidelight window and smiled. "I have a feeling it's for you."

"Me?" Lacie set her computer on the coffee table, tossed the throw aside and stood in her socked feet. Who would be here to see her? The only person she'd had contact with since she'd been back was—

Her gut tightened. Oh, please don't let it be—

"Matt, this makes twice in one day." Mom held the door, allowing him and a blast of cold air to enter. "To what do we owe this pleasure?"

Pleasure? Lacie tugged at the sleeves of her bulky sweater. That was debatable.

"Hey, Barbara." He wore a heavy coat, a pair of well-worn jeans, gloves and a black beanie. And if the hefty dose of pink coloring in his cheeks and nose was any indication, he'd walked. "I'm sorry to stop by so late."

"Nonsense." Mom closed the door behind him. "It's only eight thirty."

Yeah, never mind the fact that they were settling in for a cozy evening.

When Matt's dark gaze moved to Lacie, she noticed something different, though. His shoulders seemed to slump, as though he were carrying a heavy burden, and there was something sad in his expression. Something that made her heart go out to him, though she quickly snatched it back.

Had something happened with the play? Mrs. Nichols?

"Is Kenzie in bed?" He watched her intently.

Uncertain how she felt about this side of Matt, she crossed her arms over her chest. "Yes. Why?"

"Could we take a walk?"

A walk? Now? But it was late. Moreover, it was cold.

"We won't be long," he added.

She looked to her mother.

"I'll keep an ear out for Kenzie." Obviously the woman had read her mind.

Lacie glanced down at her computer. So much for job hunting. "Give me a sec to get ready."

She donned her coat, scarf, hat and boots, all the while trying to figure out why Matt would suddenly feel like taking a walk. With her of all people. Unless something *had* happened. Or he simply wanted to discuss his duties as director? But couldn't they do that here or someplace else that was warm?

Tugging on her gloves, she let go a sigh. She'd find out soon enough.

Outside, the air was still as they started up

the darkened street. The clouds that had plagued them all day had finally dissipated, leaving a plethora of stars in their wake. It also meant they were likely in for a very cold night. Perhaps a hot bath would be in order when she got back.

"How'd the party go?" Matt's breath hung in the freezing night air.

"Not too bad, considering there were only three of us." She stuffed her hands into her pockets. "Kenzie made out like a bandit."

"I'm guessing she'd consider it a success then." Though she didn't look at him, she could hear a hint of a smile in his voice.

"Probably."

They walked in silence for a few moments, seemingly heading nowhere in particular, which had her wondering what this walk was all about.

Approaching a dim streetlight at the corner, she said, "Did you want to discuss the email I sent you?"

He glanced her way, his expression somber. "You sent me an email?"

"I told you I would."

Again looking straight ahead, he said, "I haven't checked. Had other stuff on my mind."

Okay, then what—

Hands in his pockets, he kept walking. "I'm curious—why isn't Kenzie's father raising her?"

"What?" How dare he ask something so personal?

"I mean, typically when one parent passes, the other assumes custody."

"Unless there's a will that stipulates otherwise. Kenzie's father wanted nothing to do with her. My sister wanted me to raise Kenzie. Not that it's any business of yours."

"Were you planning to keep it a secret like Marissa did?"

"I have no idea what you're talking about. What secret?"

"That I'm Kenzie's father."

Dumbfounded, she stopped and simply stared at him. "If you're trying to be funny, you missed the mark by a long shot."

He stared back at her. "No, I'm quite serious."

Not to mention crazy. She shook her head. "Did you not pay attention in ninth grade biology? It only takes nine months to have a baby. It's been sixteen years since you and Marissa were a couple, so even if you had—"

"Marissa came to Hawaii." The intensity of his gaze heightened and bore straight into her. "The February before Kenzie was born. But then you probably knew that."

Her mind raced to keep up. Of course, she remembered her sister's trip. Marissa and Grant had just broken up for the umpteenth time.

"I was there with the navy," Matt continued. "I spent the week showing her around Oahu. And then …" He turned away as though embarrassed.

She burrowed her hands deeper into her coat. Her sister never said anything about seeing Matt. And as she recalled, Marissa and Grant got back together shortly after she returned from her trip.

February? She ticked off the months on her frozen fingers. March, April, May, June, July, August, September, October, Novem…

A sickening flurry of emotions began to churn in her belly, spaghetti and chocolate cake morphing into a lead weight. She swallowed hard as the potential reality of Matt's confession sank in.

It couldn't be true, though. Grant was Kenzie's father. He and Marissa had dated off and on for years. Until shortly before Kenzie was born, when he walked away for good.

She dared a glance at Matt, squaring her shoulders. Marissa would have told her if he was Kenzie's father. "Matt, I don't know how you came up with such a crazy notion, but I can assure you that you are not Kenzie's father."

He twisted toward her. "Really? Then how do you explain this?" He held out a five-by-seven photo. A little boy with dark eyes alight with amusement and dark brown hair that had been combed back to reveal a slight widow's peak… Just like Kenzie. "That's me at four years old. When your mother introduced me to Kenzie earlier today, I felt as though I'd met her before. I didn't get it at first. Until you told me how old she was." His voice cracked. "I'm not imagining this, Lace. I truly believe that Kenzie is my daughter."

She stared at the photo, feeling as though she might be sick. Grant was as fair-haired as Marissa had been, with eyes just as blue. Why hadn't her sister told her she saw Matt? That there was a possibility he could be Kenzie's father?

She looked away. It couldn't be true. It wasn't true. Jutting her chin into the frigid air, she glared right at Matt. "It's not true." Then, before he could say another word, she turned and ran back home.

Thanks to Lacie's abrupt departure last night, sleep had evaded Matt. Now as midafternoon approached, he was starting to feel the effects. Unfortunately, his shift wasn't over for another three hours.

Under what he would normally consider a beautiful blue sky, he maneuvered his Tahoe through the neighboring town of Ridgway, eyeing the jagged, snow-covered peaks of the Cimarrons to the east. He wanted to kick himself for accusing Lacie of hiding Kenzie's paternity, when it was obvious she was as shocked by the revelation as he was. What he couldn't figure out, though, was why she refused to believe him.

Because maybe you're not Kenzie's father.

Yet he'd gone off half-cocked with no concrete proof to back up his supposition.

Anyone could tell you were a Stephens.

The image of Kenzie's face haunted him. Wouldn't a father know his own child? After all, it wasn't like he was looking to be a dad. And while the evidence he had was circumstantial, it all added up and was impossible to ignore. At least until he had proof to the contrary.

So where did he go from here? And how was he going to convince Lacie that he wasn't crazy?

His radio went off. Possible poachers. He waited for the address, cringing when it came. He did not need this today. Or any other day, for that matter. With the mood he was in, the last person he wanted to see was his father.

Why'd he have to call while Matt was the only deputy on duty? Couldn't he have waited a few more hours for the next shift? Sure, it would be dark, but at least he'd have been off the hook.

Bound by duty, he reluctantly responded to dispatch and headed south on Highway 550. *God, I'm going to need Your help.*

Ten minutes later, his vehicle bumped across the cattle guard beneath the arched metal sign that read Abundant Blessings Ranch. He crept up the long gravel drive, praying that perhaps it had been his oldest brother, Noah, who'd made the call. Yet as he passed the recently expanded stable, his hopes were dashed when he glimpsed Noah tending the horses. He thought about stopping to check, but knew he'd simply be postponing the inevitable.

Approaching the ranch house, memories of that day nearly three years ago filled his mind. All he'd wanted to do was make Mama happy. And he had. For a short time, she'd forgotten the pain and weakness that had plagued her for months.

But Dad didn't see it that way. *Are you trying to kill her?*

Ten days later, she was gone. The cancer had finally gotten the better of her.

Just then he spotted his father exiting the new barn his brother Andrew had built over the summer.

You're nothing but a screwup, Matt. Always have been, always will be.

Clint Stephens's words didn't sting quite as much today as they had when he'd first spat them at Matt. And while Matt tried to pretend his father's opinion didn't matter, it seemed he'd been trying to disprove his father ever since. Yet for all of his trying, he'd only succeeded in proving him correct.

While Dad looked on, he parked beside the old man's dually, in front of the long wooden deck that spanned the length of the single-story cedar ranch house. Thanks to Andrew and a good power washing, the place looked almost new. The ugly black buildup from years of neglect had been whisked away. If only the damage to his heart could be so easily erased.

His father was waiting as Matt exited his truck, felt cowboy hat perched upon his graying head, hands buried in the pockets of his Carhartt coveralls. "Wondered if you'd be working today."

"I am. So whatcha got?" Because the sooner he could get away from here, the better off he'd be.

"A decapitated mule deer." The old man poked a thumb over his shoulder toward the pasture. "Near Smugglers Bend."

Matt knew the area well as he used to hunt

there all the time. There wasn't an inch on the ranch that he and his brothers hadn't explored at some point in their young lives. "I'll drive over there and walk in from the road."

His father's gaze narrowed. "He's tucked in amongst the brush. Might have a hard time findin' him, so I'd best take you."

The dread Matt had felt earlier amplified. Did Dad think he was incapable of finding it? Or that he needed a chaperone to make sure he got things right?

Whatever the case, the old man remained quiet during the ride out there on one of the utility vehicles they used to get around the ranch. Despite an abundance of sunshine, the bitter cold air stung Matt's face as they thudded over the now-dormant rangeland, carving a path around cattle and the occasional tree.

A short time later, his father brought the vehicle to a halt beside a small wooded area. Scruffy conifers and barren deciduous trees blanketed with underbrush. A hiding place for wildlife. "He was a big fella." Dad stepped off the vehicle and led Matt several feet into the thicket.

Matt eyed the once-majestic buck. "Yes, sir. But then, poachers don't make a habit of going after the little guys." He surveyed the overgrowth around the animal. "How'd you find him?"

"Neighbor called and said I had cows on

the road. When I went to get 'em, I discovered somebody had cut the fence." Dad glanced some hundred yards in the distance. "Wasn't long after that I saw the blood trail." He looked down at the dead animal. "Looks like a clean shot, though." He pointed to the entry wound behind the animal's left shoulder. "Fella never knew what hit him."

"I'm guessing they shot from the road." Matt dared a look at his dad. "Then walked in to claim their trophy."

Dad shook his head. "Them poachers are the ones that ought to be shot."

Matt took some photos and jotted down a few notes before following the trail to the road and doing more of the same. "Unfortunately, this isn't the first incident we've seen," he told his father when he returned. "I'll hand this information over to investigators, though with little to go on, catching anyone isn't likely."

They again climbed on the UTV and started back to the ranch house in silence. Matt took the opportunity to survey the land he loved so much. He gazed at the river as they passed, wishing he could spend more time there. How he used to enjoy walking the property, communing with nature, hunting, fishing… Except now he felt like an outsider. Unwelcome in his own home.

"Well, I suppose you need to get on, don't you?" His father stopped the vehicle in front of the house. "Probably have reports and such to take care of, huh?"

If Matt were anyone else, Dad would have offered him a cup of coffee. But he wasn't anyone else. No matter what he did, he was a disappointment to his father. The son who was arrested for underage drinking, then let his parents down by joining the navy without ever consulting them.

"Yes, sir."

The old man followed him to his Tahoe. "I've been hearing rumors that you're directing your mama's play."

Matt's entire body tensed. "Yes."

Hands shoved in his pockets, the old man rocked back on the heels of his worn work boots. "I gotta say, I'm kinda curious as to why you decided to do that."

Turning, he looked at his father. "They were talking about canceling the play and I couldn't let Mama's legacy die."

"I can appreciate that." Dad nodded, his lips drawn into a thin line. "But don't you think it would have been better to leave it in the hands of someone who knew what they were doing?"

Matt's blood boiled. The old man would never

cut him any slack. "Why? Because you think I'll screw that up, too?"

When his father didn't respond, Matt turned on his own booted heel. "I'm out of here." He threw himself into his vehicle, fired up the engine and exited the ranch at a much faster pace than he'd arrived.

As far as Clint Stephens was concerned, his middle son had no redeeming qualities. Just wait until he found out about Kenzie. The fact that Matt had fathered a child out of wedlock would only amplify the old man's belief that Matt was nothing but a failure, unworthy of his father's love. And as much as it killed Matt to admit it, even to himself, that's the one thing he desperately wanted.

Chapter Five

Matt could not be Kenzie's father. That's all there was to it.

Darkness had already settled over Ouray as Lacie stood at the stove in her mother's kitchen, stirring noodles into the beef Stroganoff, its savory aroma filling the air. While she welcomed the opportunity to cook for more than just herself and Kenzie, the task did little to distract her from the annoying thoughts that had plagued her brain all day. How could one brief meeting have Matt believing he was Kenzie's father? Talk about nerve.

"I'm hungry." Kenzie approached from the living room, where an educational cartoon had held her attention for the past twenty minutes.

"I know, sweetie." Lacie put the lid on the skillet, annoyed that she'd wasted most of her day, mentally rehashing last night's conversation with Matt instead of interacting with Kenzie. "How about a piece of string cheese to tide you over until Grandma gets home?"

"Okay." Her niece beamed at the prospect. "Can I play with my ponies?"

Lacie opened the refrigerator and grabbed a cheese stick. "You like those, huh?"

"Uh-huh." Kenzie nodded, accepting her snack.

She had to hand it to her mother, she'd done a good job anticipating what toys Kenzie would and would not like. "Then yes, you may. I'll let you know when dinner is ready."

"Okay." She grinned up at Lacie with a smile that reached her big brown eyes. Eyes not at all like Marissa's or even Grant's. Instead, they reminded Lacie of—

No. She shut the refrigerator door with a little too much force, rattling its contents. She wasn't going to go there because it wasn't true. Grant was Kenzie's father, even if he was a deadbeat dad.

While Kenzie played and they waited for Mom to get home from the shop, Lacie seized the opportunity to focus on something besides Matt. She crossed to the table and opened her laptop to check those job listings she'd planned to research last night before she'd been so rudely interrupted. Yet even as she stared at the computer screen, her thoughts kept returning to Matt. To the pain and conviction in his dark eyes.

She let go a groan and returned to the stove to give the Stroganoff another stir. This was ridiculous. If Matt had been Kenzie's father, Marissa would have told her. There were no secrets between them. They—

She froze. Kenzie's birth certificate. She had Kenzie's birth certificate in her files in the bedroom. Strange that she thought to keep it close by in case she needed it, yet had never taken the time to look over the document.

Quickly replacing the lid, she set the wooden spoon on its rest and started down the hall. Grant would be listed as Kenzie's father on the birth certificate, putting this nonsense to rest once and for all.

Inside her old bedroom, she opened the closet door and grabbed the plastic file box that contained all of her and Kenzie's important documents and set it on the bed. She lifted the plastic lid and fingered past shot records, guardianship papers and tax records until she located the folder labeled Birth Certificates.

She removed it from the box, opened it and read. Mackenzie Elizabeth Collier. Date of birth. Place of birth. Father...

Unknown?

Lifting her head, she stared at the glowing numbers on the bedside clock. Why would Marissa have listed the father as unknown? Did she not want Grant to be a part of Kenzie's life or—

A sick feeling in the pit of her stomach had her easing onto the same bed she'd slept in as a teenager. Grant wasn't Kenzie's father.

Her mind's eye recalled the picture Matt had shown her last night. Sure there were similarities, but that didn't mean he was Kenzie's father. A lot of people had dark hair and eyes.

And the widow's peak?

Her confusion persisted into dinner and throughout the evening. She barely touched her food. Even as she tucked Kenzie into bed, the fact that her sister had listed the girl's father as unknown not only perplexed but annoyed her. Who did that to a child?

Returning to the living room, she absently flopped onto the sofa, drawing her legs under her as she stared at nothing in particular.

"Can I get you a cup of tea?" Mom approached from the kitchen.

"No, thanks." Lacie reached for a throw pillow and hugged it against her chest.

"Care to talk about it?" Mom eased into her chair.

"Talk about what?"

"Whatever it is that's bothering you." Her

mother set her cup on the side table. "You've been in a funk ever since you came back from your walk with Matt last night."

If there was anyone she should talk to about this situation, she supposed it would be her mother. After all, she and Lacie were the only family Kenzie had left. And despite Mom's refusal to celebrate Christmas, she still cared about her granddaughter and had her best interests at heart.

"Matt has this crazy notion that he is Kenzie's father." She fixed her gaze on her sister's graduation photo hanging on the far wall. "Seems he and Marissa spent some time together while she was in Hawaii. So when he learned when Kenzie's birthday was, he automatically decided she was his daughter." She puffed out a disbelieving laugh. "He even showed me a picture of himself at the same age. As if *that* was supposed to convince me." No matter how alike they might have looked.

"Did it?"

"No." Toying with the pillow's silky fringe, she continued. "So I pulled out Kenzie's birth certificate to prove him wrong."

"And?"

She looked at her mother. "Marissa listed Kenzie's father as Unknown."

Mom drew in a long breath. "I was afraid

that might be the case." Standing, she came to sit beside Lacie.

"What?" She twisted to face her mother. "That she'd not name a father?"

"No. That Matt is Kenzie's father."

Lacie recoiled at the statement. "Why on earth would you think that?"

"Marissa told me she'd seen Matt while she was in Hawaii." Her mother rested a hand on Lacie's knee. "I know she was seeing Grant around that same time, but I also know your sister. Throw in the fact that Kenzie looks just like Matt and even I can do the math."

Lacie didn't get it. "Why didn't you say anything?"

"It wasn't my place."

"Not even after Marissa died?"

"I had no proof." Mom shrugged. "Just mother's intuition." After a silent moment, she went on. "I am curious, though." Her mother watched her intently. "Why is it so difficult for you to believe that Matt could be Kenzie's father?"

Because it means Marissa got a part of him I'll never have.

Shocked by the juvenile notion, she tossed the pillow aside and stood. What was she, back in high school? She had no interest in Matt, let alone bearing his children.

"Just blindsided, I guess." She let go a sigh

before turning back to her mother. "I mean, what am I supposed to do now?"

"You could always ask for a DNA test."

She lifted a shoulder. "I hate to put Kenzie through that."

"It's only a cheek swab." Mom stood and went to retrieve her tea. "That's hardly traumatic." Cup cradled in her hands, she eyed Lacie again. "Don't you want to know the truth?"

Lacie rubbed her arms. Only if it meant Matt *wasn't* Kenzie's father.

"Sweetheart—" her mother moved closer "—I know how much you love Kenzie. But do you think it would be fair to keep her from having a relationship with her father? Especially now that her mother's gone?"

While Lacie knew the correct answer to her mother's question, she didn't necessarily like it.

"No. But how do you even begin to explain something like that to a four—I mean, five-year-old?"

"Slowly." Mom was beside her now, cup in hand. "And probably not fully until she's older. Right now the best thing would be to let them forge a relationship. After all, she just met him."

Again, she knew her mother was right. But if Matt was Kenzie's father, where did that leave her?

She paced to the window and peered through

the blinds. "What if he wants her? What if he tries to take her away from me?"

"Lacie, Matt is a good man. Don't try to paint him as vengeful."

Turning, she said, "He thinks I knew. That I was keeping the truth from him right along with Marissa."

Mom's expression softened. "Just like you, once he has a chance to process things, I'm sure he'll realize you're telling the truth."

"But what if he doesn't?" What if he decided to fight for custody of Kenzie? What would that do to Kenzie? And what would that do to her?

By Wednesday, Matt had pulled himself together enough to know that he had to talk to Lacie again. At least to apologize for accusing her of lying. But with the majority of his shift still stretched out in front of him, he wasn't at liberty to have a lengthy conversation. That didn't mean he couldn't be proactive, though.

So shortly after ten thirty, when he knew Barbara would be at the shop, he stopped by the Collier house. He knocked on the door, praying Lacie would answer. After the way she left him the other night, there were no guarantees. One glimpse of his sheriff's Tahoe and she might pretend no one was home. Even if her SUV was still in the drive.

Just when he was thinking about knocking a second time, the door slowly opened.

Dressed in jeans and a bulky gray cable-knit sweater, Lacie clutched the knob, looking far more vulnerable than the stubborn woman he was used to butting heads with. Her caramel-colored hair was pulled back into a messy pony-tail and lines he'd never noticed before creased her forehead, as though she were just as dis-tressed about Monday night's conversation as he was. Making it even more imperative that they talk.

After a long moment, she cracked open the storm door. "What's up?"

"I was wondering if you and Kenzie would meet me at Mouse's later today. After my shift."

"I don't know, Matt. I'm pretty busy getting things ready for Thanksgiving tomorrow. Lots of cooking and such."

"It won't take long. I promise. Just give me thirty minutes."

She studied him, her gaze narrowing before she glanced back into the house, and he couldn't help wondering if she was looking at Kenzie. When she looked at him again, she let go a sigh. "I suppose I can afford thirty minutes to meet and talk about your director duties…and let you see Kenzie."

Let him see Kenzie? Did that mean she believed he was Kenzie's father?

"I get off at five. How about five thirty?"

She nodded. "That should be fine."

His hopes soared. "Okay. I'll see you then."

Excitement coursed through his body as he dashed back down the walk and climbed into his vehicle. He could hardly wait until tonight. Though he was also a little on the nervous side about spending time with Kenzie. It was one thing when he believed her just any other little girl, but now that he knew she was his own flesh and blood, his daughter, well, he wasn't quite sure what to do.

Driving away from Lacie's, he remembered Kenzie's birthday. He needed to get her a gift.

With that in mind, he headed straight for the toy store. Yet once he was inside, he found himself overwhelmed by the multitude of books, dolls, stuffed animals, games, you name it. There were things for babies and toddlers. Little kids and big kids. Outdoor toys, indoor toys.

Then it hit him. He knew absolutely nothing about Kenzie. Her likes and dislikes. What kind of toys she preferred, her favorite food, even her favorite color.

Sadness mingled with anger, twisting his gut. Thanks to Marissa, he'd missed out on everything. Every birthday, every first. So many years that could never be recaptured.

His body sagged under the weight of grief. Maybe he shouldn't get Kenzie anything. At least not until he knew her better.

He started toward the door.

"Can I help you find something?"

He turned to see Hank Marshall approaching. Hank was close to his father's age and the owner of Ouray's lone toy store. The man always claimed he loved what he did because he was nothing but a big kid himself.

"No, that won't be—"

Hank continued toward him, undeterred. "Since I usually don't see you in here, Matt, I'm guessing you're looking for a gift."

"I was, yes. But—"

"Boy or a girl?"

"Girl."

"That would explain the distressed look on your face." The older man who'd always reminded him of Mr. Rogers smiled. "How old is she?"

"Five. It's a—a birthday present." Matt swiped a hand over the sweat suddenly beading his brow.

"Well, we'll just have to find her something special."

Matt glimpsed a stack of oversize stuffed animals. "How about that stuffed dog? Do you think she'd like that?"

"For about ten minutes."

"Oh." Matt felt his shoulders droop.

"Follow me." Hank walked deeper into the store. "Kids that age want to be entertained, but they also want to be challenged. After all, they'll soon be starting school."

School? But she was so small.

Ten minutes later, Matt was feeling much better about the whole gift thing. With Hank's help, he finally decided on a set of wooden puzzle boards with pictures and letters, though, just for good measure, Matt also threw in a small stuffed kitten.

Armed with a gift bag brimming with colorful tissue paper, he exited the store, even more eager for his meeting tonight. Unfortunately, that made the rest of the day stretch on forever. Until a call came in late afternoon about an accident north of town.

He barreled down Highway 550, sirens blaring. Approaching the scene, he saw vehicles lining the road. He methodically maneuvered past them, taking in his surroundings. The sun was shining and the road was dry, so weather couldn't have been an issue. Nonetheless, traffic was at a standstill and that usually spelled bad news.

Moments later, he spotted a late-model sedan to his right, nose-first in the ditch. In the middle of the road, an older-model pickup truck sat at an angle, straddling both north and southbound lanes. The driver's-side bumper was crumpled and the headlight crushed.

He parked and exited his Tahoe as the two occupants of the car emerged with the assistance of passersby. Glancing toward the truck, he saw only one person standing guard, but making no attempt to help the person or persons inside.

By the time EMS arrived, he understood why. The elderly gentleman in the truck was deceased, though seemingly from natural causes, not as a result of the accident. According to the occupants of the sedan, the truck drifted into their lane and while they tried to swerve out of the way, the pickup struck the back end of their vehicle, sending them off the road.

In the end, the highway was temporarily shut down, the middle-aged man and woman in the sedan were treated at the scene and released and, thanks to paperwork and reports, Matt missed his meeting with Lacie and Kenzie by a long shot.

With no way to get in touch with Lacie, he went straight to the Collier house from the sheriff's office, hoping and praying that Kenzie was still awake. And that Lacie would understand.

With Kenzie's gift in his hand and his heart in his throat, he knocked on the door.

A moment later, the porch light came on, the door jerked open and a very unhappy-looking Lacie promptly joined him on the porch.

"Uh-uh. No." She wagged a finger. "You are not going to do this."

"Do what?"

"Kenzie and I waited for you at Mouse's for nearly an hour. And now you think you can just show up here and everything will be hunky-dory?" Her words rose into the chilly night air. She crossed her arms over her chest. "I will *not* let you do that to her. Not now, not ever."

"I'm sorry, Lacie. I promise you, I had no intention of missing our meeting. I've been looking forward to it all day. But there was a fatality accident this afternoon, so I got held over until just a few minutes ago."

"And you couldn't have called?" Her glare only intensified his unease.

"I don't have your number. And it wasn't like I had the time to search for your mother's."

After a silent moment, she took a step closer. "Look, even if a DNA test proves that you're Kenzie's father, you're going to have to earn the right to be a daddy. So don't think you can just step into our life and take over. Because we've done fine without you."

Staring down at her, he shifted the bag from one hand to the next, understanding her desire to protect Kenzie. But then, it wasn't as if he'd ever had a say in the matter.

Her irritated gaze lowered. "What's in the bag?"

"A birthday present for Kenzie. I picked it up this afternoon, before the call came in." And he'd been praying ever since that it was something Kenzie would enjoy. That is, if Lacie allowed him to give it to her.

"Sorry, but it'll have to wait for some other time."

He wanted to argue with her, to tell her he wasn't that kind of guy, but knew it would do no good. She'd made up her mind.

Turning, he stepped off the porch, determination coursing through his veins. No matter what he had to do or how long it took, he would earn Lacie's trust and be the dad that Kenzie deserved.

Chapter Six

Lacie pushed the door closed, leaned against it and let go a sigh. She was proud of herself for standing her ground and giving voice to those things that had been festering inside her all evening. She would not let Matt force his way into their lives and do whatever he pleased. So what if he had a valid excuse for not meeting them earlier? She was the one who'd been stuck at Mouse's with a five-year-old ogling all that chocolate.

"Who was at the door?" Mom eyed her from the kitchen.

"Matt." Turning, she peered through the sidelight. Why was he still out there?

"What did he want?" Mom tossed over her shoulder.

"He had a *g-i-f-t* for someone." Lacie had to spell out the word, otherwise Kenzie would be asking all kinds of questions. "But I told him he'd have to wait." She nudged the sheer curtain ever so slightly with her finger. Just enough to get a better view.

He hadn't even gotten into his Tahoe. He just stood beside it, staring at the ground with that stupid gift hanging from his hand.

"Why would you do that?" asked Mom.

Yeah. Would it have killed you to let him give her the present?

Straightening, she let the curtain fall back into place. She was not the bad guy here. She was simply trying to protect her niece.

You could give the guy a chance.

Huffing out a breath, she reached for the knob. "Fine." She pushed the storm door open and poked her head outside. "Matt."

When he looked her way, she motioned for him to come in.

"Thank you." His smile was one of relief as he stepped onto the porch and followed her into the house.

"Look who's here." With Matt now at her side, she closed the door and continued through the living room to the adjoining kitchen.

Kenzie popped her head up from her coloring book at the kitchen table, while Mom poured herself another cup of tea at the island.

"Always a pleasure, Matt." Mom smiled.

"Trust me, the pleasure is mine." Stopping behind the sofa, he breathed deep. "Something sure smells good. You must be cooking up a storm in there, Barbara."

"Not me." Her mother picked up her mug, bobbing the teabag up and down. "Lacie's the one who's been baking all day. Pumpkin bread, pumpkin pie…"

His attention shifted to Lacie. "I didn't realize you were so domestic."

The sincerity in his dark gaze had her looking away. "There are probably a lot of things about me you don't know." And she'd just as soon keep it that way.

She moved into the kitchen.

Matt did, too, setting his gift bag atop the island before continuing on to the table. "Hi, Kenzie."

The awe in his voice took Lacie by surprise.

The little girl paused, yellow crayon still in hand, and peered up at him. "Want to color with me?"

Seemingly nervous, he darted a glance to Lacie.

She reluctantly nodded her approval.

"It's been a long time but, sure, I'd love to color with you." He pulled out the next chair and sat down beside Kenzie. "What are we coloring?"

"I'm doing the kitty book," Kenzie explained,

"but you can color in my pony book." She dropped the crayon and pulled another book from the small stack beside her.

"I like ponies," he said.

"Me, too." Kenzie opened the book and thumbed through it before setting it in front of Matt. "You can color this horsie. He's a boy."

"Oh, I see. What color do you think he should be?"

She dug through her crayon box, coming up with two blue crayons she promptly handed to Matt. "Boy horsies are only blue."

"Really?" Practically beaming, he looked from Kenzie to Lacie and back. "I don't think I knew that."

Arms crossed over her chest, Lacie leaned against the island, watching as Matt set to work with the dark blue crayon.

She still didn't want him here. Appearances could be deceiving. What if he wasn't the good guy he seemed to be?

She felt a nudge against her elbow.

"Still skeptical?" her mother whispered.

Again focusing on the duo at the table, Lacie found it impossible to ignore the resemblance. Seeing Matt and Kenzie side by side…the hair, the eyes, the shape of their faces. Even the silly way each had their tongues peeking out of the corner of their mouths as they colored.

She hugged herself tighter. "Until proven otherwise, yes." Yet as she watched the two of them, an ache filled her heart that was as unexpected as it was unwanted. Why had Marissa never said anything? All these years she let everyone believe Grant was Kenzie's father and that he'd run out on them, robbing Kenzie of the father she deserved and Matt or whoever of the right to know his daughter.

How could her sister do such a thing? And now that the truth had been revealed, where did that leave Lacie?

Yeah, she needed to get him out of here as soon as possible. "Matt, wasn't there something you wanted to give Kenzie?"

"Oh, man, sorry. I got distracted." He pushed away from the table to retrieve the brightly colored bag. "Happy birthday, Kenzie." He handed her his gift.

Her niece's brown eyes went wide as she took hold. "For me?"

"That was pretty nice of Matt, wasn't it, Kenzie?" Mom watched from the other side of the island.

"Uh-huh." Standing on her chair, the little girl tossed the pink and orange tissue paper aside and peered into the bag. "A kitty!" She reached inside and pulled out a small gray kitten with a pale pink bow and brilliant blue eyes. "I love her!"

Hugging the toy to her chest, Kenzie looked at Matt. "What's her name?"

"She doesn't have one yet," said Matt. "What do you think her name should be?"

Kenzie scrunched her face up as she studied her gift. "Starlight."

"Starlight?" Matt and Lacie said simultaneously.

"Uh-huh." Kenzie tucked the kitten under her arm. "Her name is Starlight."

Mom shrugged, eyeing Lacie over the rim of her mug. "Reminds me of someone who insisted on naming our toy poodle Killer."

"Hey, the way he used to growl and bare his teeth…"

"There's something else in there, too." Matt pointed to the gift bag.

Setting the kitten on the table, Kenzie again reached inside the sack. "What are these?"

Lacie moved beside her for a closer look. "They're puzzles, Kenz." She glanced at Matt. "You like puzzles. And these have words and letters that will help you get ready for school next year." The perfect combination of education and fun. He'd really put some thought into his gift.

"Yeah." The little girl again picked up the kitten, tucking it under her arm.

Lacie touched her shoulder. "What do you say to Matt?"

"Thank you."

"You're welcome." The guy couldn't seem to stop smiling.

Tilting her head, Kenzie continued, "Can I play with them now?"

"Sure." Matt quickly jerked his head toward Lacie. "That is, if your aunt Lacie says it's all right."

How could she say no? Though it had nothing to do with Matt and everything to do with Kenzie. "Go ahead."

Watching Matt with Kenzie, Lacie couldn't help noticing the wonder in his eyes. But how would he feel a month or a year from now when the novelty of having a child wore off? Or when Kenzie was sick or throwing a temper tantrum? Lacie had altered her entire life for Kenzie. And couldn't imagine being without her.

"Matt—" Mom eyed him across the kitchen "—would you care to join us for Thanksgiving dinner tomorrow?"

Lacie glared at her mother. A few days ago the woman didn't even want to celebrate Thanksgiving, and now she's inviting Matt as though he's part of the family? She could have at least run the idea past Lacie first.

"Thank you, Barbara, but I have to work tomorrow."

Phew!

"Perhaps you can stop by in the evening then," Mom continued. "I'm sure we'll have plenty of leftovers."

Looked like Lacie was going to have to sit down with her mother and set some boundaries. Because the last thing she wanted to do was spend all her time with Matt Stephens. Not when being near him reminded her of the feelings she'd once had for him—and the ache of rejection when he'd chosen her sister.

While Mom gave Kenzie her bath a short time later, Lacie walked Matt to his vehicle.

"The gift was a nice gesture. Thank you."

"No, thank *you* for understanding and for letting me see her." He paused at the curb and looked down at her. "This was, without a doubt, the best night I've ever had. Kenzie is amazing."

Despite wearing her coat, she shivered in the night air. "Yes, she is."

His expression took on a more serious note. "I owe you an apology, though."

"For?" Had he lied to her about the accident? Not that she couldn't easily find out. This was Ouray, after all. Population one thousand.

"For accusing you of hiding Kenzie's paternity from me. I know that you were just as clueless as I was. And if you want me to do some DNA testing or something..."

"Yes, I plan to do that right away." Especially after seeing him and Kenzie side by side. "And just so you'll know, I'm not proud of what my sister did."

Hands shoved in the pockets of his uniform pants, he shrugged. "What's done is done. However, now that the truth is out, I have every intention of building a relationship with Kenzie. I want to be a part of her life."

"You...do know that we'll be going back to Denver after the first of the year, right?" Sooner, if she could find a job.

Looking out over the neighborhood, he nodded. "I'll do whatever I have to."

Lacie's heart nearly stopped beating. Her stomach sank to her knees.

That could only mean one thing. He was going to try to take Kenzie.

Watching Kenzie as she enjoyed a slice of pumpkin pie with him the next night at the Colliers' kitchen table only amplified Matt's knowledge that his life had been forever changed. However, he still had a play to direct. And with only three days until their first real rehearsal, he was growing more nervous by the minute.

Sure, he'd gone over the notes Lacie had sent him regarding the duties of a director, but that didn't mean he understood them. At least not completely. What he needed was to sit down with her and thoroughly discuss his role. Something he hoped to do tonight. That is, if he could get her to stick around long enough. Seemed she'd been all over this house since he arrived an hour ago, needing to take care of one thing or another. Anything except remaining in the same room with him. As though she were avoiding him.

"Are you finished with your pie, Kenzie?" Barbara brushed a hand across her granddaughter's back.

"Uh-huh."

"How about you, Matt?" The woman turned her attention to him. "Care for some more?"

"No, thank you, Barbara. I'm good." He patted his overstuffed belly, still amazed at how much turkey and dressing he'd eaten. "Matter of fact, I'm more than good."

She chuckled and took his plate along with Kenzie's and started toward the sink.

"I thought Lacie was going to be helping you at The Paisley Elk," he called after her.

"She is. I wanted to give her a few days to settle in. She'll start Saturday."

"Ah, Small Business Saturday."

"That's right." She rinsed the dishes before putting them into the dishwasher. "One of my biggest days of the year."

"What are you going to do with Kenzie?" He glanced at the child as she climbed out of her chair. "Where are you going?"

"I'm going to get my puzzles," she said before scurrying into the adjacent living room.

Her grandmother watched after her, smiling. "She'll come to the shop with us. I've got some toys and a little table there for her. I think she'll do just fine."

"It's time for somebody to get ready for bed." Lacie appeared from the hallway.

"Aww..." Kenzie frowned. "But Matt and I were going to play puzzles."

Lacie paused beside the island, perching a hand on her hip. "Sorry, Kenzikins, you've had a long day with no nap."

"But I'm not tired." The kid's words were quickly followed by a yawn.

"Yeah... I can see that," Lacie said flatly.

"I've got an idea." Barbara closed the dishwasher and moved toward her granddaughter. "How about I give you your bath again—"

Kenzie's eyes widened. "With bubbles?"

Barbara grinned. "With lots of bubbles. And what do you say we let your new mermaid doll take a bath with you."

The little girl immediately returned the puzzles she was holding to the shelf and took off down the hall. "Come on, Grandma."

Matt couldn't help laughing. "I don't think I've ever seen anyone shift gears so fast."

Shaking her head, Lacie chuckled. "You haven't seen anything yet."

"No—" he stood from the table, pushed in his chair "—but I'm looking forward to it."

Lacie's smile evaporated then. "I should probably go check on them." So she was avoiding him.

"Why?" He crossed to where she stood. "It's not like your mother hasn't bathed Kenzie before." After a silent moment, he continued, "Besides, I have something I'd like to talk to you about."

"I...really should get this food put away." She sidestepped into the kitchen.

"That's okay. We can talk while you work."

If Lacie appeared nervous before, she looked downright petrified as she picked up the plastic container of leftover turkey.

"Is something wrong?"

Her gaze jerked to his. "No. I'm just concerned about Kenzie, that's all."

"Well, I have no doubt that she's in good hands. Besides, they're right down the hall."

Lacie nodded, opening the refrigerator. "So what is it you wanted to talk about?"

"The play."

She set the turkey inside, her shoulders suddenly less rigid. "The play?" Why did she look surprised?

"Yes." Rounding the island, he picked up the casserole dish with the dressing and handed it to her. "Rehearsals start Sunday and I'm scared witless."

"Didn't you get my notes?" She tucked it away.

"I've been going over them all day. But no matter how hard I try I can't seem to wrap my brain around this whole directing thing." Pressing the foil around the edges of the pie plate, he looked her way. "You want this in there?"

"Sure." She took hold. "Then you're obviously overthinking it. Hand me the gravy, please." She pointed. "This is a small production. All you really need to do is make sure people know their blocks—"

Handing her the bowl, he lifted a brow. "Which are…?"

"Where the actors are to be onstage at any given point. You'll guide them during rehearsals, so by the time opening night arrives, everyone will have things down." She closed the fridge and, for the first time tonight, seemed to relax. "Actually, Mrs. Nichols did the lion's share of a director's job before you ever stepped into the role." Lacie grabbed a rag from the sink. "She casted the play, planned the rehearsals, established a stage manager… Now you just need to bring the play to life."

"Um—" he scratched his head "—I thought that's what the actors did."

"They do." She wiped down the island. "They bring *your* vision to life."

"My vision." He wasn't sure he had one.

Pausing, she set a hand to her hip. "Have you seen *The Bishop's Wife*?"

"Are you kidding? I've been watching the movie at least once a day since I agreed to direct."

"Good. That should give you a basic understanding then." Returning to the sink, she rinsed the rag and turned off the water. "About those actors, though." She faced him now. "I think it might be best if I step down. I only have a minor role, so someone else could easily cover it."

What little hope had begun to take root vanished. "What? Why would you do that?"

She shrugged, grabbed a pot holder from beside the stove and tossed it into a drawer. "With all that's happened this week, things that have come to light, I just feel like it might be awkward."

"Not for me, it wouldn't." Panic morphed into a plea. He took hold of her arms. "I'd be lost without you, Lace. I can't risk messing this up." The intensity of his words had him quickly letting go. How had he come to depend on her so quickly? As though she were his compass, pointing him in the right direction. Just as she'd been back in school, before he'd lost his way.

"You keep saying that." She looked at him curiously. "I understand that you don't want to fail your mother, but…why are you so afraid?"

Was it that obvious?

Scratching his head, he turned away. After the conversation with his father the other day, his fear of failure was probably greater than ever. But did he dare share that with Lacie? Reveal the chinks in his already loosely held-together armor?

At this point, he supposed he had nothing to lose. Not if he hoped to talk her into continuing on with the play.

He drew in a deep breath before facing her again. "My dad and I aren't on the greatest of terms. Matter of fact, we barely speak at all."

"But I thought the two of you were close. I mean, you worked alongside him at the ranch."

"That was a long time ago." He met her

gaze. "Nowadays, he thinks I'm nothing but a screwup."

"Aw, Matt, we all have issues with our parents, but I'm sure—"

"He blames me for my mother's death."

Her mouth formed an O before she pressed her lips together.

Taking a couple of steps, he glanced down the empty hallway before saying any more. "She had cancer and we knew she was nearing the end." His attention shifted back to Lacie. "Dad was out working cattle and Mama was all alone when I came into the house. We visited for a while and she mentioned that she wanted to see Chessie, her horse. It was a nice day. Warm, no wind, so I carried her out to the barn. Even set up a chair for her so she could spend some time without getting worn out."

Arms crossed, Lacie leaned her backside against the counter. "I do remember how much she loved the horses."

He couldn't help smiling. "Yes, she did. And it made her happy to be near them again. But when Dad walked into the barn and saw Mama, well, he wasn't happy, but he kept his cool. At least until Mama fell asleep later. Then he asked me to meet him in the barn. When I did, he went off on me."

Her brow puckered. "What did he say?"

Spotting the forgotten container of cranberry sauce, he picked it up and passed it to Lacie. "He was furious that I'd brought her outside. Accused me of trying to kill her, when all I wanted to do was make her happy."

"Of course you did." She watched him over her shoulder as she again opened the fridge.

"She died the following week. Dad told me that I was nothing but a screwup, pointing out all the things I'd done wrong in my life. Everything from the underage drinking incident after graduation, even though the charges were dropped, to leaving the ranch behind and joining the navy without even consulting him, then getting kicked out—"

"You were kicked out of the navy?" Closing the door, she looked at him.

Why had he said that? "I punched a guy who'd had too much to drink and was getting aggressive with a woman. Problem was, he was one of my superior officers. So I ended up having to choose between a reduction in rank or a general discharge. I took the discharge."

"How long ago was that?"

"Almost five years. Shortly after my mother got sick."

"All because you were trying to help someone?"

"Yeah, well, that's not how my father saw it."

"What did he say?"

"Nothing. He simply shook his head and walked away." Matt raked a hand through his hair. "I can only imagine what he'll have to say when he learns I fathered a child out of wedlock."

She was back against the counter. "When are you going to tell him?"

"The question isn't when, it's *if*." Suddenly weary, he started toward the door. "Tell Kenzie I said good-night."

"What do you mean *if*?" Lacie followed him. "Suppose you are Kenzie's father. Is that something you're ashamed of?"

He lifted his coat from the rack, feeling as though he couldn't get anything right. "No." Looking down, he saw the fire in Lacie's eyes. "I could never be ashamed of Kenzie. Just my actions, that's all."

She continued to glare at him before finally looking away.

He couldn't blame her for not trusting him. Though he really wished she would.

Arms crossed, she studied the carpet. "Well, you don't have to worry about the play."

Hope ignited. "Are you saying you'll stay?"

She met his gaze. "Not only am I going to stay, I'm going to see to it you put on the best play this town has ever seen."

Chapter Seven

Lacie entered the Wright Opera House Sunday afternoon, wishing she had kept her big mouth shut.

I'm going to see to it you put on the best play this town has ever seen.

What had she been thinking? One week ago, she rued the sight of Matt Stephens. Now she'd barely gone a day without seeing him. And even after he'd said he would do whatever he had to in order to be with Kenzie.

Lacie knew good and well what that meant. Yet she'd thrown away her only opportunity to bow out of the play. All because he was a wounded soul who wanted to make his mother—and father—proud. Sure, he and his father were estranged, but behind that angry facade, Matt wanted nothing more than to earn his father's approval. And like a fool, she said she'd help him.

Continuing past the box office, she took hold of the theater's original walnut railing and stormed up the stairs, thankful for the burgundy-and-gold carpet that muted the thudding of her boots. She needed to have her head examined.

Or better yet, she needed to find a new job and fast. One that would get her away from Ouray well before December 25. Otherwise, she'd never be able to give Kenzie the Christmas she deserved.

What about Matt?

She'd worry about that *if* and *when* they confirmed he was Kenzie's father.

On the second floor, she peered out the expanse of windows that overlooked Main Street. The sights and sounds of Christmas were all over town, while she and Kenzie were trapped at Scrooge Collier's house, where even the mention of the holiday was sure to bring a swift admonishment.

No kid should have to live like that.

She huffed out a breath. For today, though, she had to make it through the first play rehearsal. Not to mention four subsequent rehearsals in as many nights, culminating with performances Saturday and Sunday. Then she could finally be rid of Matt Stephens. Or, at least, no longer forced to be around him. When it came to Kenzie, though, she had a choice.

Inside the lovely old theater, she took off her coat and draped it over the back of a chair before adjusting the sparkling red scarf looped around her neck. Her mother might not celebrate Christmas, but she definitely did.

Pretending to dig for something in her purse, she discreetly surveyed the space to see who all was there. She recognized Larry Garcia, Valerie and several of the other cast members. The stage manager and, of course, Matt.

"Hi, Lacie." Clare waved as she approached from the back of the room, her long golden brown hair swaying from side to side with each movement. "How was your Thanksgiving?"

"It was good." Lacie set her purse on the chair. "How about you?"

"Crazy." Clare rolled her eyes. "All my nieces and nephews running around. My dad and brothers arguing over a football game."

Lacie tried not to laugh. While Clare might not have appreciated all that family time, Lacie would love nothing more than to be surrounded by such chaos. The way it used to be when she was young.

"Are you ladies ready to get this show on the road?"

She and Clare turned to see Valerie coming toward them. Close to Lacie's mother's age, the spunky brunette was always quick with a smile and never had a bad word to say about anyone.

"I can hardly wait." Clare, who was playing the lead role of Julia, slipped off her coat, practically bubbling with excitement.

Lacie knew how she felt. She always loved the start of a new project. Her gaze inadvertently drifted to the stage where Matt was talking with the guy in charge of the lighting. Of course, back in Denver she didn't have to work with a director who posed a threat to her on more levels than she cared to admit.

Fortunately, he seemed more interested in a successful play than zeroing in on her, so as rehearsal got under way she relaxed and began to enjoy herself. Acting was definitely a therapy for her. Escaping reality and pretending to be someone else. The fact that they were doing one of her favorite plays didn't hurt, either.

The community theater she was a part of back in Denver had put on *The Bishop's Wife* last December and Lacie had been fortunate enough to be cast in the lead role. It was the biggest role she'd ever had and was quite the undertaking, but one she would never regret. Especially with the turn her life had taken since then. This would mark the first time she'd acted since Kenzie came to live with her.

Two hours later, with a successful rehearsal behind her, Lacie met with the stage manager to discuss her costume fitting before gathering her things.

"So how'd I do?" Matt took her coat from her hand and held it up for her.

After a hesitant moment, she shoved in one arm then the other. "You did great." She shrugged the coat over her shoulders and pulled her hair from beneath the collar. "All that time you spent watching the movie and poring over the script came through in your attention to detail."

He winced. "I hope I wasn't too overbearing."

"Not at all."

"Good." He visibly relaxed. "How was your first day at the shop?"

"Surprisingly enjoyable." She buttoned her coat. "We were quite busy."

"Kenzie do okay?"

"Yeah, she had a great time." Something Lacie was more than grateful for. "You wouldn't believe what she did, though." She rested a hand on her hip. "Mom and I were both busy assisting customers, so when another lady came in, Kenzie decided to help. She marched right up to the woman and—"

What was she doing? Rattling on as though she and Matt were doing this parenting thing together. As though he were a part of their lives. So what if he was Kenzie's father? She was the guardian who'd given up everything for a child she loved more than she'd ever thought possible.

Not that that would count for much in a court of law. If Matt sued for custody of Kenzie, how could Lacie ever win?

"Go on." Matt's smile was full of anticipation. "What did she do?"

Lacie's gaze fell to the wooden planks beneath her feet as she pressed a hand against her stomach to quell the rising nausea. "I'm sorry. I'm suddenly not feeling so well."

He took a step closer, the concern in his dark eyes unnerving. "Are you okay? Would you like me to drive you home?"

"No." She picked up her purse. "I'm sure I'll be all right. I just need to lie down for a minute." *And get away from you.*

"In that case, you definitely don't need to be driving. Why don't you give me your keys? I'll drive you, then come back for my Jeep."

"No, really. That's not necessary. Kenzie isn't even home. Mom took her with her to Montrose."

"This isn't about Kenzie, it's about you."

She eyed him suspiciously, recalling the caring boy she once knew. The one who put others before himself and always looked out for his friends. Unlike her sister's, which was purely superficial, Matt's heart was what made Lacie fall in love with him all those years ago.

"I'm not taking no for an answer, Lace." Placing a hand on her shoulder, he turned her around and propelled her toward the exit. "Now let's get you home."

Matt was growing weary of Lacie's stubbornness. Particularly when her face was so pale and it was obvious she needed help.

So despite her objections, he not only took her home and escorted her inside the house, but he was determined to stay until her mother and Kenzie got home. He wanted to see for himself that she was, indeed, going to be okay.

"This is so unnecessary. You don't have to stay." She argued from the couch. "A little herbal tea and I'll be fine."

Arms crossed over his chest, he stared down at her. "Well, you're wrong. I do have to stay. However, if you'll point me in the direction of the tea, I'll be happy to fix it for you."

She huffed out a breath and looked the other way. "Never mind."

"Sorry, no can do." Whisking past her, he made his way into the kitchen and put the kettle on to boil. "Now let's see, if I were an herbal tea bag, where would I be?" He opened the cupboard next to the stove. Nope.

"You're not funny," she said.

"I wasn't trying to be." He moved on to the cupboard near the coffee maker. Score! "Man, who knew there were so many different kinds of tea?" He riffled through the plethora of boxes, locating two that said Herbal. "Which one do you want? Chamomile or ginger peach?"

"Surprise me."

A few minutes later, he returned to the sofa and handed her a steaming mug. "I decided on the ginger since it's supposed to be good for stomach problems."

She looked at him suspiciously. "How do you know that?"

"I just do." Curiosity had him wandering toward a grouping of photos on the white bookshelves against the far wall. "Oh, and be careful, it's hot." He studied a picture of Lacie and Marissa as little girls and another of them with their father when they were teenagers.

Lacie had always been more reserved than her sister. So he'd been pleasantly surprised the day she barreled up the drive of the ranch in her father's Jeep. Even if it was for nothing more than to rub in the fact that she'd gotten her driver's license before he did. Still, he liked that she'd wanted to share that momentous occasion with him.

That kind of stuff stopped after he and Marissa started dating. And though he'd never acknowledged it at the time, he missed Lacie and the camaraderie they'd once shared. She got him in a way no one else ever had.

On the next shelf, he spotted a photo of Marissa in a hospital bed, smiling and holding a newborn.

His heart twisted as he picked it up and touched a finger to Kenzie's face. *I wish I could have been there.*

Clearing the emotion that suddenly clogged his throat, he returned the picture to the shelf and went to check on Lacie.

"How is it?" He picked up the purple throw draped across the back of the sofa and laid it over her stretched-out legs before sitting down on the ottoman opposite her.

"It's fine."

Resting his forearms on his thighs, he clasped his hands together. "There's something I'd like to ask you. I'm just not quite sure how to do it."

She stared into her cup. "Just say it and get it over with." Her words held an air of defensiveness.

"I've heard the stories of how Marissa died,

that she was in a car with some guy when it crashed, but…where was Kenzie?"

Finally, she looked at him, her expression softening as it so often did whenever her niece was the topic of conversation. "She was spending the night with me. Something I have thanked God for many, many times."

The corners of his mouth twitched. "Did that happen often? Kenzie staying with you." He wasn't trying to interrogate her, he simply wanted to know about Kenzie's life.

"Sometimes more often than others." She set her cup on the side table. "I never minded, though. I've loved her as though she were my own from the moment she was born." She adjusted her blanket. "I had the privilege of being Marissa's birthing coach."

"So Kenzie has known you all her life?" Something he wished he could say.

"Yeah." She met his gaze with an intensity that hadn't been there before. "There's not much I wouldn't do for that little girl."

"I know." He stretched his legs out in front of him, crossing them at the ankles. "She's blessed to have you, Lacie. Not everyone would be willing to take on the role that you have."

She lifted a shoulder. "I don't know. I think I'm the one who's blessed. There's not a day that goes by that I don't thank God for her."

"Me, either." The words seemed to fall out so naturally. Probably because they were true. "At least not since I found out about her."

Silence fell between them for so long he was afraid he'd offended her. Then again, in her eyes, he was the guy who posed a threat to something she held very dear.

"About that DNA test." She must have read his mind.

And while he knew in his heart that Kenzie was his, he understood Lacie's need for proof.

"I ordered a test kit."

He lifted a brow. "Ordered?"

"Thought that would be the most discreet way to handle this. I'll need a cheek swab from both you and Kenzie to send to the lab. We should have the results by the end of the week."

"Is it reliable?"

"One hundred percent accurate, according to the website."

Restless, he pushed to his feet and started to pace. "I want you to know that I'm not a love-'em-and-leave-'em kind of guy." He probably shouldn't have said that, but for some strange reason, it mattered what Lacie thought of him.

She lifted a shoulder. "We all make mistakes."

"I tried to stay in touch with Marissa, but she never answered my calls." He again dropped onto the ottoman. "When she finally did, she told me that she and her boyfriend were back together, so I shouldn't call anymore." Head in his hands, he stared at the carpet. "I didn't even know she had a boyfriend."

"That must have hurt."

"It did. Made me feel—"

"Like you'd been used."

For a moment he thought she was chastising him. But lifting his head, he saw only understanding in her eyes. "Something like that, yeah."

Sitting straighter, she reached for her tea. "Marissa rarely thought about anyone but Marissa." She took a sip, then cradled the cup in her hands. "I'm not saying she was a bad mother. She loved Kenzie and doted on her. But...there were times when I worried about my niece's safety."

His whole body tensed. His hands fisted. "Did she hurt her?"

"No, Marissa would never do that. But with so many men moving in and out of her life, I...had some concerns."

He knew exactly what she was talking about. "I would, too." An unexpected anger filled his words. "Sorry, that wasn't directed at you. Just the situation."

"I understand. There were times I was pretty upset myself." She set her feet to the floor.

"Kenzie should have been Marissa's top priority, not Marissa."

Looking at Lacie now, he couldn't help wondering how two sisters could be so different. One self-serving, the other self-sacrificing. And while most people thought Marissa the prettier of the two Collier girls, he was beginning to see that Lacie's beauty far outshined her sister's. Hers wasn't superficial. Instead, it emanated from inside her, touching those around her.

Including him.

Chapter Eight

Lacie really needed Matt to leave.

This conversation was getting way too intense. Not only had he managed to get her to open up, sharing things she'd never shared with anyone else, she'd also seen the pain that flickered in his dark eyes when he talked about Marissa and the way she'd just cast him aside. Something Lacie had witnessed firsthand on more than one occasion. Why was it always the good guys her sister hurt?

Yes, despite being sucked in by her sister, Matt was one of the good guys. To Lacie's chagrin. Because for as much as she wanted to dislike him, she couldn't bring herself to do so. Not when he was still the same caring guy she'd once lost her heart to.

However, she did not need or want a man in her life. Especially one who held the power to take away the one thing she cherished most in this world.

So she practically jumped for joy when she heard the garage door open. "Sounds like Mom and Kenzie are back."

Thank You, Lord.

Matt stood as the door leading from the kitchen to the garage burst open a few moments later.

"Matt!" Kenzie cheered when she spotted him. She charged across the room, her light-up shoes flickering, and stopped right in front of him.

"Hey, there, small fry," he said, looking down at her.

She giggled. "Want to play puzzles with me now?"

His smile reached from ear to ear. "I live to play puzzles with you."

The kid giggled again. Did he have her wrapped around his finger or what? Or maybe it was the other way around.

Unfortunately for Lacie, though, it meant he wouldn't be leaving right away.

She tossed the throw off her legs and stood as her mother entered, carrying several plastic bags and a massive pizza from the supercenter deli.

"Let me help you, Mom." Grateful for the distraction, she hurried into the kitchen and took hold of the bags.

"Thank you, dear." Her mother set the un-baked pizza on the counter. "Matt, I didn't know you were here. I'm glad I decided to get the larger pizza."

He strode toward them. "Lacie wasn't feeling well after rehearsal, so I wanted to make sure she was okay."

Mom's gaze shifted to Lacie. "Are you all right, dear?"

Not that she was ever really sick. At least, not in the way Matt thought.

"Yes, I'm feeling much better now thanks to Matt and some ginger tea."

"Good," said Mom, turning on the oven. "Ginger is always helpful for an upset stomach."

Matt nudged Lacie with his elbow. "See."

"Come on, Matt." Kenzie tugged on his other hand. "Let's play."

Mom looked at the two of them. "It would appear that you're in high demand around here, Matt."

"I wouldn't have it any other way." He winked at Lacie before heading around the island to join Kenzie at the table.

Unexpected heat crept into her cheeks.

Perhaps *she* should consider leaving.

She didn't, though, and even after Matt had

gone home and she helped Kenzie into bed later, thoughts of her time alone with him continued to play through her mind like a sappy movie. The way he'd insisted on taking care of her, even when all she'd really been was heartsick, had her feeling a bit guilty. No one had paid her that much attention in a long time. And while she didn't want to like it, she did.

With Marissa's old Strawberry Shortcake lamp glowing on the night stand, Lacie sat on the edge of the bed as Kenzie pulled her princess comforter up to her neck.

"We seed Santa Clause at the store."

"You did?" Lacie brushed an unruly strand of dark hair away from the child's face.

"Grandma wouldn't let me say hi to him, though."

"Well, maybe we can say hi to him later."

Kenzie pouted then, her brow puckering as she crossed her arms over her chest. "She wouldn't let me look at the Christmas trees, either."

Lacie's heart squeezed. How she wanted this Christmas to be extra special for Kenzie. Unless her mother had a change of heart, though… "Grandma was probably in a hurry to get home."

"But we need a Christmas tree so it can be Christmas."

Lacie swallowed the lump that lodged in her

throat. "Kenzie, Christmas is in our hearts. Not in a tree or the decorations. Sometimes we forget that Christmas is Jesus's birthday."

"He was a little, bitty baby." Kenzie sounded like a baby as she held her hands close together.

"That's right."

"But then He growed up to be big." She thrust her arms wide. "Like Matt."

Lacie couldn't help chuckling. "He did."

Kenzie again snuggled under her covers and yawned. "I like Matt."

Lacie thought about all she'd discovered about him today. "Want to know a secret?"

Kenzie nodded, her eyes wide.

"I like him, too." Making it even more imperative that she keep her distance. Although, considering they had rehearsals the rest of the week, that was going to be a challenge.

Smiling, Kenzie held her arms up for a hug.

"Good night, sweetie." Lacie hugged her tight. "I love you."

"Night, night."

Out in the hallway, Lacie closed the door and drew in a deep breath.

Oh, God, I know Christmas isn't about trees, decorations or gifts, but I so want Kenzie to be able to experience all of the joy this special season has to offer. Please, soften Mom's heart and allow her to see things through her grand-daughter's eyes.

With Kenzie's words still ringing in her ears, she continued down the hallway and into the living room.

Mom sat in her chair near the window, reading as usual. She glanced at Lacie as she entered. "Everything okay?"

"Yeah." Pausing behind the sofa, she dug her fingers into the plush throw. "Can I get you some more tea or anything?"

"No. I just poured a fresh cup, so I'm fine."

While her mother went back to reading, Lacie rounded the end of the couch, mustering all of the courage she could find, and sat down. "Mom, I'd like you to reconsider having a Christmas tree for Kenzie. She's just a little girl. Next year, you can go back to—"

"We already had this discussion, Lacie." The woman never even looked up. "I have deliberately chosen *not* to celebrate Christmas."

Lacie willed herself to remain calm, though everything inside her was screaming. "No, you've deliberately chosen to be mad at God for taking Daddy. Do you really think you're going to get back at Him by refusing to celebrate His Son's birthday?"

Without even flinching, her mother finally met her gaze. "I really don't care what God thinks." Then she went back to reading her book. Or at least pretending to.

Lacie's ire did spark now. She shot to her feet, hands fisted at her sides. "I'm sorry you feel that way, Mom. However, I am going to do everything in my power to make this the most special, most amazing Christmas that Kenzie has ever seen."

Mom lowered her book and took off her readers. "There will be no Christmas tree in this house." Her voice was firm, yet even. "No decorations, *no* celebrations."

Lacie thought of her father, her bottom lip trembling. He was the godliest man she'd ever known. One who reveled in the holidays, sharing the good news of Jesus with everyone he came in contact with. "Daddy would be so disappointed in you."

Turning on her heel, she walked to her room and dropped onto the bed, a flurry of emotions darting through her. *God, what am I going to do?*

Matt stood in front of the Collier house Friday evening, filled with gratitude. Not only were rehearsals finally over, Lacie had received the results of the DNA test today, proving beyond a shadow of a doubt that he was, indeed, Kenzie's father. A sense of pride wove through him.

He had a daughter. Now if he could just survive this weekend's performances.

Unfortunately, all of the rehearsals this week hadn't allowed him much time with Kenzie. Just a few minutes here and there. So tonight he was looking forward to taking her and Lacie to the town's Christmas tree lighting. The annual event was one of his favorites of WinterFest. Carols, hot cocoa and, of course, the lighting of the tree. He couldn't think of a better way to start the holiday season.

With a spring in his step, he headed up the walk. But before he even made it to the porch, the door flew open and Kenzie bolted toward him in her coat, snow pants and winter boots.

"Matt!" She threw her arms around his legs and squeezed with all her might.

The gesture nearly knocked him over, both physically and emotionally. The way she'd so readily accepted him. He couldn't remember the last time he'd felt so much love or had someone so genuinely happy to see him. He could definitely get used to this.

He lifted her into his arms. "That was some greeting."

"I misseded you." She patted his cheeks, the look in her eyes as sincere as it was innocent.

"I missed you, too, small fry."

She giggled then, a sound he would never tire of hearing, and hugged him around the neck.

"Where's your aunt Lacie?" His breath hung in the chilly night air.

"Right here."

He and Kenzie both turned to see her coming toward them, wearing a light gray puffer jacket over a pair of jeans, a white scarf and a white knit cap.

"You look great." Then again, she always looked good.

"Thank you." Pink tinged her cheeks. "Just trying to keep warm. Which reminds me—" she pulled a small pair of gloves from her pocket "—we need to put your mittens on, Kenzie."

The child held out her hands, allowing Lacie to assist her.

"Are we ready now?" He set Kenzie to the ground.

"Yes!" she cheered.

Lacie tugged on her own gloves. "I believe so."

Through the cold night air, the three of them proceeded the few blocks to the center of town, Matt on one side of Kenzie, Lacie on the other, each holding her hand. Almost as though they were a family. They walked along the sidewalk, past homes with inflatable snowmen and Santas in their yards, others with light displays and most with Christmas trees in their front windows.

"Are you guys getting ready for Christmas yet?" He hadn't thought much about it, but was excited that he'd get to spend this one with his daughter.

"No." Lacie kept her gaze fixed straight ahead, her expression flat. "We've been busy at the shop this week."

"Well, we're barely into December." He shrugged. "You still have plenty of time."

"Hey, Matt," he heard as they rounded the corner onto Main Street.

Turning, he saw his brother Andrew, his wife, Carly, and their ten-year-old daughter, Megan, coming up behind them.

"I thought that was you." His brother looked surprised. Probably because he was used to seeing Matt alone.

"I wondered if you'd be here." Matt's gaze moved from Andrew to Carly. "You remember—"

"Lacie…" A smiling Carly moved in for a hug, her blond curls peeking out from beneath her knit hat. "I haven't seen you in forever." She released her. "When did you get into town?"

He'd forgotten the two women knew each other. Carly had been a couple of grades ahead of them, but everyone knew everyone at Ouray's only school.

"Last week. Kenzie—" Lacie nodded toward her niece "—and I are helping Mom at the store for a while."

"Oh, you two will have to drop by some time then, so we can catch up." Carly touched her daughter's shoulder. "Megan, this is my old friend Lacie."

Bundled up in a purple puffer and purple hat, her strawberry blond hair splayed around her shoulders, his niece smiled.

"Hi, Megan," said Lacie. "This is Kenzie."

While the females continued to chat, Megan and Kenzie becoming fast friends, Matt took a step back with his brother.

"That's Marissa's daughter, right?" Andrew studied the little girl and Matt couldn't help wondering if his brother could sense that same familiarity he'd had when he first met Kenzie.

"Yes." He leaned closer. "And mine, too."

Andrew stared at him, confused, before looking to Kenzie and back again. "She's your daughter?" he whispered.

"I'll fill you in later." He kept his voice low. "Suffice to say, I only recently found out. Yes, Lacie knows, but Kenzie does not, so mum's the word."

"You got it, bro." A still-looking-stunned Andrew patted him on the back. "Congratulations."

His heart swelling with pride, Matt rejoined the women. "Hey, we'd better get on down to the tree lighting before we miss it."

They continued along the street, Lacie and Carly chatting all the way, as were Megan and Kenzie, until they reached the corner of Main and 7th Avenue. The still-darkened Christmas tree was surrounded by revelers singing "We Wish You a Merry Christmas."

Each of the adults and Megan were handed a piece of paper with the words to the songs they'd be singing. Megan shared hers with Kenzie, even though Kenzie didn't know how to read. Still, he appreciated the gesture.

After a couple more carols and some hot chocolate to chase away the chill, the mayor thanked everyone for coming then started the countdown to the lighting.

"Ten, nine…"

"This is it." Matt lifted Kenzie into his arms so she could have a better view. He could tell by the way she kept looking around that she wasn't quite sure what was going on.

Lacie must have noticed it, too. Taking hold of Kenzie's hand, she pointed to the tree. "Look, sweetie. They're going to turn the lights on."

"Three, two, one—"

Cheers erupted from the crowd, but Matt kept his gaze fixed on Kenzie.

Her gasp and wide eyes when they flipped the switch were priceless. "I want a Christmas tree like that." She pointed.

"Pretty cool, huh?" He joined his fellow townsfolk in a round of "Oh, Christmas Tree" until he felt Lacie beside him.

"Watch Kenzie for me." The distressed look on her face tore at his heart. And as she turned to walk away, he was pretty sure he saw tears in her eyes.

What could have happened? Had he done something wrong?

Whatever it was, he had to find out.

He caught Andrew's and Carly's attention. "Would you two mind keeping an eye on Kenzie for a few minutes? I need to check on Lacie."

"Is everything okay?" asked Carly.

"That's what I intend to find out." He set Kenzie to the ground. "I need you to stay with Megan and her parents for a few minutes. I promise, I'll be right back."

"Can I have more hot chocolate?" She held out her empty cup.

Carly took hold of it. "Of course you can." She eyed her daughter. "Come on, Megan. Let's get some more cocoa."

Matt scanned the area, looking to see where

Lacie had gone. Finally spotting her across the street, he made his way to her.

Her back was to him, so he moved in front of her to discover she was crying.

"What's wrong?" He instinctively put an arm around her.

"I'm sorry." While people continued to sing behind them, she dabbed at her face with a tissue. "It's just that Kenzie was so happy."

"And that's a bad thing?"

"No." She sniffed. "But I wanted to make this Christmas special for her and I can't."

Because she'd lost her job. "Lace, if this has to do with money, I'm more than happy to—"

"No, it's not the money." She drew in a breath. "It's my mother." She looked up at him. "She hasn't celebrated Christmas since my dad died and she's not willing to make any exceptions."

He continued to watch her. "Not even for Kenzie?"

Lacie shook her head. "She refuses to let us have a tree or anything that even remotely resembles Christmas."

"That's crazy."

Her tears were gone now. "No, that's a bitter woman who's mad at God."

No wonder Lacie was so upset. Kenzie was just a kid. And this would be her first Christmas since her mother died. Of course her aunt wanted to make it special.

For that matter, *he* wanted to make it special. He couldn't let his little girl not have a Christmas. Especially when it was the first one he'd get to spend with her.

He laid his gloved hands atop Lacie's delicate shoulders. "All right then, we'll just have to do Christmas at my house."

"Your house?" Her pretty gaze searched his.

"Yes." And the more he thought about it, the more he liked the idea. "We'll have to wait until the play is over, but maybe Monday we can all go to Montrose. We'll pick up a tree and some decorations and we'll give Kenzie the best Christmas a kid could ever have."

He felt her body relax.

And the smile she sent him reached deep inside, warming every part of him.

"Kenzie is one fortunate little girl."

"Yes, she is." He touched a finger to Lacie's cheek. "Because she's got the best aunt ever."

Chapter Nine

Opening night had arrived. Matt wasn't quite as nervous as he'd thought he would be. Still, he prayed things would go well. He did not want to shame his mother's legacy.

Backstage, he fingered the burgundy velvet curtain just far enough apart to watch as people arrived. There sure were a lot of them. Young and old, families…and he knew almost every one of them.

He continued to observe, his chest tightening when he saw his father enter with Hillary Ward-Thompson, an old schoolmate of Dad's that he'd recently become reacquainted with. Now Matt was nervous. The only thing worse than failing would be failing in front of Dad.

"I need you, Matt." Corey Winslow, the play's stage manager, scurried across the wooden floor, looking even more rattled than Matt felt.

He let the curtain fall closed and turned to face her. "What's wrong?"

"It's Clare." He never knew Corey was such a nervous Nellie.

His gaze narrowed. "What about her?"

The petite brunette sucked in a breath. "She's sick." The woman cringed. "She can't go on."

Can't go on? How could they perform *The Bishop's Wife* without the bishop's wife?

So much for not being nervous. Between this and his father, Matt's anxiety level just went through the roof.

He shoved both hands through his hair as he started to pace. "This is not good." What was he going to do?

"No, it's not," said Corey. "But at least we have a backup."

He whirled to face her. "We do?" Why didn't he know that?

"Yes. Lacie did this same show last year and played the role of Julia."

He stared at his stage manager. "Well, why are you standing here then? Why aren't you telling her all of this?"

Corey smiled and nodded. "Because that's your job."

"Oh." Lacie must have left off that portion of a director's job description. "Where is she?"

Corey shook her head. "She's here somewhere."

He took off, nearly running into Lacie as she exited costuming in her maid outfit. "Lace—" he gripped both of her arms "—I need you."

"What?" She quirked a brow.

"I mean, get back in there. You need to change."

She glanced down at her costume before again looking at him. "Okay, why don't you take a deep breath and tell me what's got you so stirred up?"

Behind him he could hear the audience growing larger, while backstage people were running around like chickens with their heads cut off.

He let go a sigh. "Clare is sick and can't go on. Would you *please* take over as Julia?"

"Oh, no. I hope Clare is all right." She pressed a hand to her chest. "But yes, of course, I'll take over."

He nearly collapsed with relief. Instead, he hugged her like he'd never hugged anyone before. "Thank you, Lace. Thank you."

"Don't you think I'd best go get changed?" Her words were muffled against his shoulder.

He quickly released her. "Yes, definitely. Go change." Turning, he lifted his gaze to the century-old hand-hewn rafters. "Thank You, Lord."

A short time later, he watched from backstage as the house lights went down, feeling a bit like the captain of the *Titanic*. "Here we go."

He wasn't sure he breathed again until the closing lines were uttered. But the cast had done it. They'd pulled off a flawless performance.

The audience applause was overwhelming. Everyone was on their feet as the cast was introduced, though the loudest applause was for Lacie. And rightfully so. Without her, they wouldn't have had a play at all.

Then he was called onstage. Still standing in the wings, he looked all around. Nobody had informed him he'd have to do that. He was a behind-the-scenes kind of guy.

Next thing he knew, Lacie and Valerie Dawson were at his side. They each took hold of an arm and escorted him center stage as the crowd continued to applaud.

Blinking, his gaze again drifted upward. *I hope you approve, Mama.*

Once the introductions were complete, the cast and crew descended the stage to greet those in attendance. Matt shook hands with everyone who passed, overwhelmed by the number of people congratulating him on a job well done.

"That was wonderful, Matt." Dressed in a stylish pantsuit, her short blond hair perfectly styled, Hillary clasped both of his hands. "I'd forgotten how much I loved that movie, but you brought it all back. Thank you."

"You're welcome. I'm glad you enjoyed it."

"See you at the diner?" She tucked her short blond hair behind one ear.

"Wild horses couldn't keep me away."

She winked and continued down the line.

Then his father stepped in front of him. "The troop did a fine job. Your mama would be proud."

Matt hated the disappointment that wove through him. The ache he felt in his heart. He knew what Mama would have thought. Even if the play had flopped, she would have been proud, because she was always proud of her boys no matter what they did.

But Dad? No, he wasn't proud. If he was, would it have killed him to say so?

Unfortunately, all the praise Matt had received did little to overshadow his father's remarks. Even as he finished putting the props away ninety minutes later, the pain lingered.

"One down, two more to go." Lacie was kind enough to stay and help him.

"If I survive." He shoved the bishop's desk into a corner.

"What are you talking about?" She perched a hand on her now-denim-covered hip. "The play went off without a hitch."

"Thanks to you." He came alongside her. Taking hold of the maid's broom she had yet to put away, he stared into her beautiful blue eyes.

With one hand still on the stick, she studied him a moment. "What's wrong?"

"Nothing."

"Then why are you so bummed?"

He took the broom from her and laid it atop the desk as she gathered up her things. "I don't mean to sound ungrateful. I know that the play was a hit."

Still watching him, she put on her coat. "But...?"

He shrugged into his own jacket as they started for the door. "I'd really hoped I could make my father proud. But he wasn't impressed."

After pausing to turn off the house lights, they started down the stairs.

Lacie remained beside him. "Did he say that?"

"Not in so many words." On the main level, he held the door for her then locked up before joining her on the sidewalk. "He just said that Mama would be proud."

"Matt, that doesn't mean he's not proud." She continued beside him as they moved toward their vehicles. "Maybe he just doesn't know how to express it."

"I wish that were true." His steps slowed.

"It appears we both have issues with our parents," she said.

"Sure looks that way. Let's just hope we never do that to Kenzie." Thoughts of his daughter lifted his spirits.

Lacie stopped and stared at him, though her expression was unreadable. "You're forgetting... I'm not Kenzie's parent."

How could she even think such a thing? After all he'd learned about her, what he'd witnessed. She was more of a parent than a lot of folks in this world.

"Yes, you are." Standing there in the cold, their breaths swirling together, he touched her cheek. "You're the best mother my little girl could ask for." And a pretty good match for him, too, he was starting to discover.

His gaze fell to her lips. Beautiful lips. Lips that spoke truth and love.

She took a step back then. "I need to go."

Lacie hung up her costume in the prop room after their final performance Sunday afternoon. She'd have to do a better job of steeling her heart against Matt. Though it wasn't easy when he looked at her with those velvet-brown eyes that beckoned her to let him in. Like he'd done last night.

Still, for Kenzie's sake, she couldn't let down her guard. She'd vowed she'd have no men in their lives and that's how she intended to keep it.

Matt isn't any guy. He's Kenzie's father.

But what if she opened herself up to him and things didn't work out? What if he was just using her to get to Kenzie?

No, she wouldn't put herself or Kenzie through that. And with this year's play now in the record books, she couldn't wait to get home and have a quiet evening with her niece.

Returning to the storage-closet-turned-dressing-room to gather up her things, she ran into Valerie.

"Lacie, it sure would be nice if you could stay in Ouray." Valerie picked up her coat. "You've been a great addition to our team."

The compliment warmed her heart. "Thank you, Valerie. Unfortunately, there's not much of a market for interior designers in Ouray."

"No, but there's always Telluride." The woman's green eyes glimmered. "Have you checked with any of the builders over there?"

Telluride. She hadn't even considered it. But it was less than an hour's drive from Ouray. "No, I haven't."

"Something to keep in mind."

Out of the corner of her eye, Lacie saw Matt approaching.

"Great job, everyone."

"Thanks, Matt." Lacie, Valerie and a couple other cast members responded in unison.

He motioned Lacie toward the stage.

Reluctantly, she joined him.

"Hey, what do you say I take you and Kenzie out for a celebration dinner?"

She glanced at the wooden floor. "Actually, I was thinking a quiet evening sounded kind of nice, after all the busyness here." Maybe he'd get the hint.

"Yeah, I guess you're right." He paused, hands on his hips. "So what if I pick up pizza instead and we hang out at your mom's? Maybe watch a Christmas movie— No, I guess that won't be happening. Unless you want to grab Kenzie and come on over to my place."

This time of year, Lacie loved nothing more than curling up with a good Christmas movie. Just not with him.

"So what do you say?" Under the bright lights, he shifted from one foot to the other. "I mean, we need to do something to celebrate me surviving the play. Not to mention your incredible performance." And then he had the nerve to look shy. "Besides, I'd really like to see Kenzie for a little bit."

"We'll all be together most of tomorrow, you know? That is, unless you forgot about the decorations."

"I didn't forget. I just miss her when I don't get to see her for a while." He shrugged. "Oh, and if you two come to my house, maybe you can get a better feel for what we might need in the way of decorations."

Why was it so hard to tell him no? Then again, he was letting them have Christmas at his house. And while it may not be ideal, it was all she had and, for that, she was grateful.

She adjusted the coat draped over her arm. "Kenzie likes cheese pizza."

He grinned. "I remember that from last Sunday at your mother's. But what about you? What's your favorite?"

"I'm a supreme kind of girl."

"A woman after my own heart."

If only things were that simple.

After getting his address, she went by her mother's to pick up Kenzie, who was beyond excited about going to Matt's house. Realizing that her niece might get bored, Lacie paused to gather up some coloring books and crayons, reading books, as well as the puzzles Matt had given her for her birthday, and then they were on their way.

Though it was dark outside when she eased to a stop in front of the 1905 two-story craftsman-style home, the lights illuminating the expansive front porch revealed the charm of a bygone era. Matt had said the house was a fixer-upper but, as a designer, she saw a lot of potential. Even if she had yet to see the interior.

"Can I ring the doorbell?" Standing on the porch, Kenzie looked up at her.

"Yes, you may. But only once." As opposed to over and over, which she was fond of doing. "We don't want to give Matt a headache."

"Come on in," he said a few moments later.

They entered into a spacious living room with beautiful dark wood floors and a coffered ceiling. Against the far wall, the original fireplace was flanked by gorgeous glass-front wooden bookcases topped with simple leaded-glass windows.

"Matt, this is incredible." Christmas music played softly in the background as she moved farther into the room, wanting to take it all in. Despite the heavy use of dark woods, the space still felt cozy and inviting thanks to the light-colored furniture and walls.

"Thanks." He moved beside her, holding Kenzie's hand. "Stripping off all of that old paint was a labor of love."

Lacie jerked her head in his direction. "You mean all this wood was painted?"

"Multiple times." He frowned.

"So you stripped and refinished all of this?" Talk about time-consuming.

"It took forever, but yes."

She looked him in the eye. "I must say, I'm very impressed."

"Well, before you get too excited, I should tell you that this and the dining room are the only ones I've finished. The rest is a work in progress."

"Don't sell yourself short, Matt. Anything worthwhile takes time."

He watched her for a moment. "I'll have to remember that." Then with a smile, he said, "Now who's ready for pizza?"

"Me!" Kenzie bounced up and down, her shoes flickering.

Five minutes later, Lacie stood in the opening between the kitchen and living room, holding her plate with two slices of supreme and Kenzie's plate with one slice of cheese, all the while eyeing Matt's light taupe furniture. And even though there was a coffee table…

"You're sure you want us to eat in the living room?"

"Why not?" Standing behind her holding his plate, he continued. "I do it all the time."

Lacie tossed a glance over her shoulder. "Yeah, but you're not five."

"Oh. Good point." His gaze shifted to the other opening that led into the dining room.

"But if we're at the table we can't watch the movie. So...how about I grab a blanket for Kenzie and she can have a picnic on the floor in front of the TV?"

"That should work." She looked down at Kenzie. "But we need to keep our drinks in the kitchen, okay?"

"Okay." The kid nodded.

After Kenzie was settled, Matt picked up the television remote. "So let's see what's on."

Within seconds, *Rudolph the Red-Nosed Reindeer* appeared on the screen.

Sitting cross-legged atop the old comforter Matt had spread on the floor, her little mouth full of pizza, Kenzie straightened. "I want to watch this."

Still standing, Matt sent Lacie a questioning look.

She shrugged. "I watch it at least once a year anyway."

"Yeah, me, too." He set the remote on the coffee table and picked up his plate. "So where do you think we should put the tree?" He took a bite.

"I don't know." Making her way past Kenzie, she stopped beside him. "Where did you put it last year?"

"I didn't have a tree last year." He peered

down at her. "Which is why we need to go buy one."

"I see." She set her plate down and moved about the space to get a better feel for things. "How about over there—" she pointed toward the corner "—against the wall, beside the bookcase? That way you can see it wherever you're sitting, but it won't be too close to the fireplace."

"Hey, who am I to argue with a designer?" He took another bite.

"And the mantel would look beautiful with some lighted greenery." Remembering this wasn't her home, she added, "Unless you think it's too much."

"No, I like that look."

His approval had her biting her lip. When did things get so easy between them? Like they'd been back in high school. Like this was the way they were meant to be.

She quickly shook off the crazy notion. She and Matt were not meant to be.

Before the show was over, but after she'd finished her pizza, Kenzie pulled a book from the tote Lacie had brought and handed it to Matt. "Will you read this to me?"

He looked at the cover. "*Goodnight Moon*. I remember this book. Sure, I'll read it." He took a seat on the couch. "Hop on up here."

From across the room, Lacie watched as Kenzie climbed into his lap and snuggled against his broad chest. Definitely one of the sweetest sights she'd seen in a long time.

As Matt started to read, she gathered their plates and took them into the kitchen, then rinsed their glasses. When she returned to the living room to fold the blanket, Kenzie was asleep.

Lacie moved toward the pair. "Would you like me to take her?"

"No." He never took his eyes off his daughter. "I just want to look at her." And he did, for what seemed like forever, as though trying to take in every little nuance.

"She really is a great kid," he finally said.

"You'll get no argument from me there."

It was obvious that Kenzie was growing attached to Matt, making Lacie feel bad about taking her back east. Every little girl needed a daddy. And Matt had already missed so much time.

There's always Telluride. Valerie's words echoed in Lacie's mind.

A job in Telluride would mean she and Kenzie could stay in Ouray. Though it would also mean spending a lot of time with Matt, fighting to keep her feelings in check.

Or you could let them go and see where things lead.

Except that was a risk Lacie wasn't sure she was willing to take.

Chapter Ten

Matt knew that he loved Kenzie. But holding her last night, watching her as she slept, her little body relaxed against his in complete trust… He'd never been more enamored.

So if Lacie wanted Kenzie to have the perfect Christmas, then Matt intended to do everything in his power to make that happen. Even if it meant spending half the day with a bunch of crazed holiday shoppers. At least they'd come on a Monday instead of the weekend.

Christmas music echoed overhead as he pushed the supercenter shopping cart past a small forest of artificial trees. Green trees, white trees, some with fake snow. Some had white lights while others had multicolored ones and still others had no lights at all. Fat trees, skinny trees…

"I like the pink one," said Kenzie.

A pink Christmas tree? He shook his head. Definitely not like the real ones he and his family used to have at the ranch.

His mother would spend months wandering the land, scoping out the perfect tree. Then, shortly after Thanksgiving, they'd hitch a trailer to the tractor and the whole family would go out, cut it down and bring it home. He could still remember how the house would be filled with the scent of fresh pine.

"That is cute." Holding Kenzie's hand, Lacie knelt beside her and admired the pint-size tinsel tree. "But it's pretty small." She grinned up at him. "Matt might trip over it."

Kenzie looked from the tree to Matt as though considering Lacie's advice. After a moment, she said, "We need a *big* tree." She held her arms wide.

"That's right, small fry." He ruffled her soft curls. "The bigger the better."

"Okay, then." Laughing, Lacie pushed to her feet, looking pretty cute herself in her glittering snowman sweater.

"I can't believe I let you talk me into coming out here with everybody and his brother."

Matt's smile faded. He knew that voice.

"Oh, don't be such a stick-in-the-mud, Clint. Where's your Christmas spirit?"

And that one.

He turned, doing a double take when he spotted his father and Hillary standing a few feet away, also looking at Christmas trees.

He inched the cart forward. Perhaps he could pretend he hadn't seen them.

But Lacie nudged him with her elbow. "Are you going to say something or should I?"

Just then, Hillary looked their way, her smile instantaneous. "Well, hello, you two." While Dad scowled at him from behind a flocked faux fir, Hillary continued toward them, wearing a stylish sweater and jeans that had definitely come from a much pricier store than this one.

"Lacie, right?" Hillary shook her hand. "We met after the play."

"Yes, I remember. It's good to see you again, Hillary."

The woman's gaze fell to Kenzie. "And who do we have here?"

Lacie placed her hands on the girl's shoulders. "This is Kenzie."

Hillary introduced herself. "Are you getting a Christmas tree?"

Kenzie leaned into Lacie and nodded.

"Hey, Clint," said Lacie as he approached. "How are you?"

The old man tilted his dirty beige felt Stetson farther back on his head and glared at Hillary.

"I'd be a lot better if someone hadn't dragged me all the way to Montrose to pick out a tree."

Matt's gaze shot from Hillary to his dad. "You're getting a tree? But you always cut a fresh one at the ranch."

"Wasn't planning to do one at all, but Ms. Fancy Pants over here says I have to." Dressed in his usual Wranglers, denim work shirt and Carhartt jacket, the old man poked a thumb toward the trees. "At least one of these prelit things ought to be a lot easier."

Easier, yes, but not how Mama would have done it. How could Dad even think about an artificial tree? What about tradition?

So why are you thinking of getting one?

Matt glanced at a superskinny tree. Good question. Of course, until a couple of days ago, he hadn't been planning on having a tree at all. Still, why had his first thought been to go out and buy something fake instead of cutting down the real deal? Especially when this was his first Christmas with Kenzie and both he and Lacie wanted it to be extra special.

"I pointed the ranch out to Kenzie on our way here," said Lacie.

Her shyness abating, Kenzie took a step forward. "I want to see the horsies."

The old man smiled and crouched to her level. "You do?"

Matt's insides tensed. He and three of his brothers looked like his father. And Kenzie was definitely a Stephens. Would his father see the resemblance? Would he figure out that Kenzie was Matt's daughter? His granddaughter?

Kenzie nodded, her brown eyes sparkling, completely unaware that the man she was speaking to was her grandfather.

"Then you need to tell Matt here to bring you on by."

Kenzie's face rivaled the lights on the Christmas trees beside her. "Can we go now?"

"Sure." Dad stood. "We just need to grab us a tree then we're headed right back." Shoving his hands into the pockets of his jeans, he looked from Matt to Lacie. "What do you two have going on?"

"We need to pick out a tree and some decorations," said Lacie.

"But that shouldn't take us too long," Matt was quick to add. Not when he had something in mind that would be far more fun than spending the afternoon at a superstore. Because if they were going to give Kenzie the best Christmas ever, he was going to make sure they did it right.

"Tell you what, let's forget about these phony things." Matt gestured toward the colorful array of plastic and tinsel. "Why don't we all head back to the ranch, let Kenzie see the horses and then I'll cut down a *real* tree for both of us?"

Lacie's smile grew wider by the nanosecond. "I *love* that idea."

"Oh, it does sound like fun, doesn't it?" Hillary clasped her hands together. "Maybe the three of you could even stay for lunch. Clint's got a pot of chili waiting for us at the ranch house. And with the way he cooks, I'm sure there's enough for a small army."

He looked at his father now. "So what do you say, Dad?"

The old man's gaze narrowed. "Shouldn't you be workin' today?"

"Nope. I've got the day off."

His father grunted. "What about them poachers? You got any leads yet?"

Matt tried not to let his father get to him. "No, but the investigators are working hard to find them, and I'm sure they'll be in touch with you soon."

"Come on, Clint." Hillary elbowed him. "It's not like Matt was volunteering you to cut down any trees."

Matt bit back a chuckle. He was growing to like Hillary more all the time.

"Don't know how we'd get it back." Dad scraped a worn cowboy boot across the concrete floor. "Trailer's got a flat."

"I can fix it." Matt wasn't sure if the old man was being ornery in general or because it was Matt who had made the offer. Either way, this wasn't about him. It was about his daughter's Christmas.

His father shifted from one foot to the next. "Them real trees, though, they can get kinda messy. You gotta keep adding water and such."

Surely the old man could come up with a better excuse than that. "Dad, since when have you ever had anything but a real tree?"

No response.

"Okay, fine." Matt took hold of the cart. "I'll just cut one for us then."

That seemed to get his father's attention. "Now, you don't need to go gettin' all cranky."

He was being cranky?

"Clint—" Lacie took a step toward him "—if you don't want us to cut down a tree from the ranch, it's okay. I understand."

His father's expression softened. "I never said I didn't want you to." His gaze briefly shifted to Kenzie. "'Course, we can't let the little one down. She wants to come see the horses."

The kid grinned. Obviously she'd won Dad over.

He looked at Matt, his countenance more resigned than argumentative. "Guess we'll see you back at the ranch."

* * *

Excitement bubbled inside Lacie over the unexpected turn of events. She was so glad they had run into Clint and Hillary. Otherwise, they would be back at Matt's now, decorating an ordinary tree. Instead, they were bumping across the rangeland of Abundant Blessings Ranch in a utility vehicle towing a flatbed trailer, in search of the perfect Christmas tree. And giving Kenzie an experience she was sure to remember.

She looked down at her niece, who was tucked between her and Matt on the lone bench seat, and tightened her seat belt. "What did you think about those horses, Kenzie?" In the open-air vehicle that reminded her of a cross between a dune buggy and a small truck, she had to raise her voice to be heard over the engine.

"They were big." Not nearly as big as her smile, though.

Lacie appreciated the way Matt had lifted Kenzie into his arms, making the massive animals less intimidating for her as he patiently introduced each one.

"Yeah, like the tree we're gonna get, right, Kenzie?" Holding tight to the steering wheel, a grinning Matt nudged the girl with his elbow.

She nodded, adjusting her pink knit cap with her mitten-covered hands.

Lacie eyed the cottonwoods lining the riverbank in the distance. Backdropped by conifer-covered, snow-capped mountains, the scene reminded her of a rustic Christmas card. All it needed was a light-adorned evergreen somewhere and it would be perfect.

"I'm so glad you suggested this, Matt. Hunting for a real tree is beyond anything I could have dreamed of for this Christmas."

"Good." He grinned, his camo ball cap shading his face from the afternoon sun. "I kind of like the idea of making your dreams come true."

Despite the chilly temperature, her cheeks warmed. Seemed he was doing just that, first by offering to give Kenzie the perfect Christmas at his place, then again today. His actions were enough to have gratitude and excitement twisting and tangling into one overwhelming emotion. An emotion she had no business feeling when it came to any man. Except he wasn't just any man. He was Kenzie's father.

Talk about complicated.

Over her shoulder, she glimpsed Clint and Hillary following behind them on another UTV. "So what's the story with your dad and Hillary?"

"I'm not sure." Matt veered northward, his expression taking on a more serious air. "I know they were friends in high school. She left Ouray, but recently moved back to be near her daughter and grandkids." He glanced her way. "Do you remember Mrs. Ward and the Miner's Café?"

"Yes."

"That was Hillary's mother. Hillary's daughter Celeste now owns Granny's Kitchen. She married Gage Purcell." Gage was an old schoolmate of theirs.

She shoved her gloved hands between her knees for the added warmth. "Talk about full circle."

"I've got to admit, it was pretty weird seeing Dad and Hillary together at the store like that."

"Why?"

He shrugged. "She's not Mama."

"I see." If there was one thing she knew for certain, it was how much each of the Stephens boys adored their mother. "Well, is Hillary a bad person?"

"No." The corners of his mouth tipped upward again. "Actually, from what little I've been around her, she's pretty good at putting the old man in his place. As you witnessed today." He made a sharp turn.

Laughing, Lacie grabbed hold of the roll bar to keep her from sliding into Kenzie. "I suspect Mona would approve, then."

"I'm still surprised Dad wanted to come with us." Matt eyed the rearview mirror as though checking on the vehicle behind them. "After the way he tried to deter me earlier. As if cutting down a tree was the stupidest thing he'd ever heard."

"Don't take it personally."

"How can you say that? Even Hillary came to my defense."

"Yes, but I don't think his avoidance had anything to do with you. I think it's because it reminds him of your mother."

She knew she'd struck a chord when he didn't respond. He simply blinked, continuing to stare straight ahead.

"Bringing in the Christmas tree was something you always did as a family, right?"

He nodded. "Mom picked it out and Dad would cut it down."

"So without Mona at his side, it's not the same. I mean, think about it, Matt. They were married for how long?"

"Forty years." He brought the vehicle to a stop near a wooded area. "You might be right, Lace." He turned off the ignition and reached an arm across the back of the seat to squeeze her shoulder. "Thanks."

Between the warmth of his touch and the intensity of his gaze, her heart pounded.

Finally, his focus shifted to Kenzie. "Now let's go find us a tree."

"Yay!" Kenzie couldn't unbuckle her seat belt

fast enough, so Matt helped her as Clint and Hillary pulled alongside them.

Clint killed the engine. "You sure this is where you want to look?"

Matt grabbed the chain saw he'd put in the bed before they left the house. "Mama always seemed to find some good ones in here." He eyed the wooded area. "Since it hasn't been touched in a few years, thought there might be something worthwhile."

"Let's give it a go, then." Clint climbed out of his vehicle.

The five of them moved into the woods where barren deciduous trees mingled with junipers, firs and pines.

"Look, Kenzie." She saw the wonder in her niece's eyes. "This is way better than the store, isn't it?"

The little girl nodded.

"But unlike the trees at the store," Matt said, "no two are going to be the same. They could be tall and skinny, short and fat, full, skimpy... you just never know."

Hands buried in her pockets, Lacie continued beside him. "I'm not sure what I'm looking for exactly, but I'll know it when I see it." Something full, perhaps, but not too wide, with a straight trunk.

"That's how it usually goes, Lacie." Clint's

voice echoed from behind them. "You know it when you see it."

Kenzie gasped then. "Look at this." She picked up a pinecone as though she'd found the greatest treasure ever.

"Pretty cool," said Lacie.

Squinting against the sun, the child peered up at her. "Can I keep it?"

"If it's okay with Mr. Clint."

"Sure you can," he said.

Leaves crackled beneath their feet and snow remnants crunched as they moved deeper into the thicket. Overhead, a couple of magpies chattered back and forth.

"That's a nice one there, Clint." Hillary approached a squatty blue spruce. "You said you didn't want a big one."

Matt's father moved closer and circled the tree that didn't quite reach his six feet. "Don't see any big holes." He stepped back, continuing to scrutinize the conifer in question. "I believe it'll do."

"Oh, good." Hillary appeared especially pleased.

"Well, that was easy." Matt approached with the chain saw.

"Everyone get back," hollered Clint as the saw roared to life.

Within seconds the tree crashed to the

ground. The women watched as Matt and his father loaded it onto the trailer.

"Looks like it's our turn, Lace." Matt rejoined her and Kenzie.

Along with Clint and Hillary, they resumed their search and in no time Lacie was eyeing a substantial Douglas fir. Not too fat at the bottom, perfectly tapered…

"This one looks good," she and Matt said in unison.

How about that? They actually were in agreement.

Except when she turned, she saw that Matt was looking at an entirely different tree. And while it was still a Douglas fir, it was way too wide with branches so close together it would be hard to place the ornaments.

"I think this one over here would fit in your living room better." She pointed to her tree.

"Are you kidding? That's way too skinny."

"No, it's not. Sure, it's not fat like that tree—" she aimed a finger at his selection "—but at least there's plenty of room for ornaments."

"What are you talking about? Do you see all those branches?" He took hold of his tree. "You can get a ton of ornaments on there."

"But your tree is flat on top," she continued. "How are we going to put the star on?"

"Trust me. The star will fit just fine." He

looked at his father and Hillary. "What do you two think?"

Arms crossed, Hillary lifted a shoulder. "I'd have to go with Lacie's tree."

"What?" Clint frowned. "Look how full Matt's tree is."

Matt swiped a hand through the air. "Forget it. There's only one person whose opinion really matters. Kenzie, what do you think?" He turned to the spot where she had been.

Lacie's heart dropped. "Where's Kenzie?" She jerked her head right and left, scanning high and low.

"She was just here." Matt looked every bit as stricken as she felt. He set the chain saw to the ground. "Kenzie?"

"Oh, no." Lacie gripped his arm. "The river."

Eyes wide, he looked at his dad and Hillary. "Stay here in case she comes back. Come on, Lace."

Turning, they ran in the direction of the river.

Blood roared in Lacie's ears. Tears stung the backs of her eyes. Why had they not seen Kenzie wander away?

Conviction pricked her heart. *Because you were so consumed with finding the perfect tree that you weren't paying attention.*

A sob caught in her throat. *God, help us find her. Please, let her be okay.*

Her foot caught on a branch and she fell flat. Air whooshed from her lungs.

Matt helped her up, his expression more panicked than she'd ever seen. "You okay?"

"I'm fine. But we have got to find—" Over Matt's shoulder she spotted Kenzie. "There she is."

He turned. "Oh, thank God."

They rushed to her side.

"Kenzie, sweetie." Lacie dropped to her knees, trying to catch her breath. "We didn't know where you were. You're not supposed to run off like that."

"Are you all right?" Matt asked.

"Uh-huh." She smiled as though she didn't have a care in the world. "I finded the perfect Christmas tree." Her little finger pointed.

Both Matt and Lacie turned to find a tree unlike either of the ones they had chosen. The blue spruce was spindly and misshapen with more bare spots than branches. And while it wasn't quite a Charlie Brown Christmas tree, it was far from perfect.

Matt glanced from the tree to Lacie to Kenzie, then back to the tree. "That's the tree you want?"

"Uh-huh," said Kenzie.

He looked at Lacie.

She shrugged, knowing that she would have

done just about anything for Kenzie right now. "If it's the one she wants…"

"I hear ya." His smile echoed Lacie's relief. "I'll go get the chain saw."

Chapter Eleven

After a lunch of chili and corn bread at the ranch, Matt, Lacie and Kenzie returned to his house to decorate their tree. Lacie helped him carry it into the house, set it up and now, as he finished stringing the multicolored LED lights they'd bought in Montrose, she pulled a pan of break-and-bake cookies from his oven. After all, what was a tree-trimming party without cookies and cocoa? Even if they were both instant. She just hoped the decorations would perk up that sad little tree.

Not that she or Matt really cared anymore. Today was all about Kenzie.

"Cookies are done," she hollered from the kitchen.

"So are the lights," Matt responded.

Perfect timing.

She quickly transferred the cookies to a plate then joined Matt and Kenzie in the living room.

He knelt beside the tree, in the corner, near the bookcase as they'd discussed last night. "Are you ladies ready?"

"Yes!" they responded in unison.

Hand perched on her hip, Kenzie looked rather impatient. "Hurry up, Matt."

He laughed. "Okay, here we go."

A split second later the humble tree glowed with brilliant shades of red, green, blue, yellow and orange.

Kenzie gasped, tilting her head all the way back so she could see the top of the tree that almost reached the nine-foot ceiling. "Pretty."

"And we're not even done yet, small fry." Matt joined them at the coffee table. "Your aunt Lacie is going to add some of that ribbon we bought, then we get to put on the ornaments."

She stared up at him very matter-of-factly. "Don't forget the star."

"That's right." He lifted Kenzie into his arms and started back toward the tree. "And since you're going to put it up—" he hoisted her over his head "—we'd better make sure you can reach."

Laughing, she stretched out an arm as he moved her closer. "I toucheded it."

"Good." He lowered her into his arms again.

"Then you got the job, kid. Now, what do you say you and I chow down on some of those snowman cookies while Lacie puts the ribbon on the tree."

"Okay." She wriggled free.

Armed with a large spool of burlap ribbon and scissors, Lacie moved toward the tree. "You guys had better leave me some."

"Aww, do we have to?" Matt handed a cookie to Kenzie.

"Yes, you have to."

"Man. You hear that, Kenz? The boss says we can't eat all the cookies."

Her niece scrunched up her nose. "You're so silly, Matt."

Watching the two of them, one would think they'd known each other forever. Kenzie seemed as comfortable with him as she was with Lacie. And Matt…?

The look of horror and desperation on his face when he realized Kenzie was missing was unlike anything Lacie had ever witnessed. And it said a lot about the depth of love he felt for his daughter.

But not only had he been there for Kenzie, he'd been there for Lacie, too. She couldn't imagine what she would have done without his help. Then again, if it weren't for him, she and Kenzie wouldn't have been there in the first place.

She glanced up at the tree. Nor would they be here, getting ready to decorate and celebrate this most wonderful time of the year. And considering the fact that Kenzie was completely unaware anything bad had happened, things still looked pretty special in her eyes. Meaning their goal had been achieved.

When she'd finished adding the ribbon to the tree, she stepped back to inspect.

"Hey, it's looking better already." Matt came alongside her and she inhaled the aroma of fresh air and chocolate.

Talk about a powerful combination.

"Thanks." Setting the remaining ribbon and scissors on the table, she eyed Kenzie enjoying the last of her hot chocolate—in the living room, no less. Definitely a special occasion. "Looks like we're ready for the ornaments."

Kenzie carefully set her cup down on the coffee table then grabbed the massive container of shatterproof ornaments they'd bought at the store. Shiny balls, glittering balls, red ones, silver ones, some with candy cane stripes… And light enough for a five-year-old to carry.

Matt turned on some Christmas music and suddenly Lacie felt as though she'd been transported back in time. The tree trimming, the cookies and cocoa, the music… Just like when she was little and her family would gather.

Now Kenzie would have those same memories. Thanks to Matt.

When all of the ornaments had been placed on the tree, Lacie removed the glittering silver star from its packaging. "This is all that's left."

"That's your cue, small fry." Matt lifted Kenzie into his arms as Lacie handed her the topper. "You're going to stick it on top of this branch right here." He pointed.

"Okay."

Lacie readied the camera on her phone as Matt lifted Kenzie into the air.

Click. Click.

"I did it," said an excited Kenzie as Matt returned her to the floor.

"You sure did." Lacie knelt beside her. "And it's perfect."

Matt took a step back. "Actually, it really is." He motioned for Lacie join him.

"Well, I'll be." If she hadn't seen it, Lacie never would have believed that between the ribbon and the ornaments, this once-pathetic-looking tree was more perfect than anything she'd ever seen.

She held up her phone and snapped another picture. "You two get over there now."

They did and she took a couple more shots.

"Hey, do you have a timer on that thing?" Matt asked.

She glanced at her phone. "I think so. Why?"

"So we can get one of all three of us."

She located the timer, he set the phone on the TV stand and lined up the shot, then they all hurried to get into place in front of the tree. Matt and Lacie on their knees with Kenzie standing in between.

The flash went off.

"Let's see what we got." She hurried to retrieve her phone with Matt at her side. A couple of taps and there on the screen was a perfect picture of all of them and their perfect tree.

"I like it," said Matt.

So did she. Perhaps more than she was willing to admit, even to herself. They looked like a real family. A notion that sounded better every time they were together. Matt's attentiveness to Kenzie was undeniably attractive. Especially when he turned that same attention toward Lacie.

Just then, her phone rang and her friend Jill's name appeared on the screen.

"Sorry." She glanced at Matt.

"You go right ahead," he said. "Come on, Kenzie, let's pick out a Christmas movie."

"Hey, Jill." Phone pressed to her ear, Lacie moved into the kitchen.

"Lacie. Oh, how I've missed you." Jill had also been one of her coworkers.

"Aww, thank you, Jill."

"I'm serious." She could envision her friend pouting. "Work isn't near as fun without you."

She eyed the darkening sky outside the window over the sink. "It's not like it was my idea to leave."

"I know. But I heard some news I wanted to pass along to you."

Lacie straightened. "What is it?"

"I was talking to another designer who told me about a builder down in Colorado Springs who's looking for someone."

"Really?" She leaned against the counter. "The housing market is booming there."

"Which is why they're in need of someone with experience."

"Well, I definitely have that." Almost a decade's worth. And while she'd hoped to find something in the Denver area so she could keep Kenzie in the same daycare with her friends, perhaps this was God's way of nudging her in a different direction. Considering she'd already given up her apartment… "This could be just what I'm looking for."

She took down the info. "Thanks, Jill. I'll give them a call tomorrow."

She ended the call with a renewed sense of optimism. Yet when she returned to the living room and saw Matt and Kenzie cuddled up on the couch, staring at the TV, something twisted inside her.

Perhaps what she was really looking for was right here in Ouray, after all.

Matt came in from work the next day, smiling when he caught sight of the Christmas tree. Aside from that brief scare with Kenzie, it had been one of the best days he'd had in a long time. Even Dad hadn't been able to dampen his spirits. Then Lacie told him about that job in Colorado Springs.

He strolled across the room and plugged in the lights. Even if he lived to be a hundred, he'd never forget decorating this first tree with Kenzie.

Taking the phone from his pocket, he pulled up the images Lacie had sent him last night. Kenzie and him in front of the tree. Him, Lacie and Kenzie. He stared at the photo. How could Lacie even consider a job on the other side of the state? Sure he understood that she needed a salary and that her given career field was better served back east, but that would mean separating him from Kenzie when he'd already missed out on so much. Didn't that count for something?

He zoomed in on Lacie's image. Truth was, he didn't want either of them to go.

A knock sounded at his door, stirring him from his thoughts. He wasn't expecting anyone, but maybe Lacie and Kenzie had decided to surprise him. Or simply wanted to see their tree. He crossed the living room and swung open the door only to find his father standing on the other side.

Matt's smile evaporated. His entire body tensed. Dad had never come to see him before. Had never even set foot in Matt's house. So what was he doing here now?

After a long moment, his father said, "Mind if I come in?"

Still at a loss for words, Matt stepped back, allowing the man entry.

Continuing into the living room, Dad removed his cowboy hat, revealing his thick salt-and-pepper hair. "Tree looks nice."

Matt closed the door and followed him, still suspicious. "Thanks."

"Your brothers tell me you've done a lot of work on this place." He scanned the space. "Don't know what it looked like before, but I'd say you've done a pretty good job."

"Yeah, well, there's still plenty left to do." He peeled off his tactical vest and set it on the floor. "What can I do for you?"

The old man turned to look at him with those dark eyes Matt had come to appreciate as much as fear. "There are a few things that have been bothering me."

Great. What had he done now?

Matt crossed his arms over his chest. "Such as?"

The muscle in his father's jaw twitched. "Tell me more about little Kenzie."

If Matt thought he was nervous before… "What would you like me to tell you?"

Dad thumped his hat against his denim-clad thigh. "For starters, are you her father?"

For a moment, Matt couldn't breathe. His lungs constricted, tighter and tighter. Digging deep, he willed his pulse to a normal rate. "How did you figure it out?"

"'Cause she looks like a Stephens." The old man glanced away then. "Actually, I couldn't shake the feeling that I'd seen her before. Then, when I mentioned it to Hillary, she's the one who asked if you could be Kenzie's father." He glared at Matt now. "I'm guessing she was right."

Lowering his arms, he took a step closer as though daring his father to do something. "Yes, Dad, she was. Congratulations, your screwup son fathered a child out of wedlock."

The old man never flinched. Didn't bat an eye. "No. My son has a daughter."

Matt couldn't have felt more off balance if

his father had hit him with a left hook. He narrowed his gaze. "What did you say?"

"I owe you an apology, Matt. One that's long overdue."

He blinked as years of pent-up emotions rose to the surface.

"You're no screwup, son. I am."

Matt swallowed the lump that lodged in his throat.

"I was mad that I was losing your mama and needed to lash out." Dad's dark eyes shimmered. "Unfortunately, I took it out on you. Seeing those horses made your mother smile. Yet I let you believe that I held you responsible for her death. And I can't tell you how sorry I am."

Still blinking, Matt stared at the coffered ceiling to keep his tears from falling. He felt as though he were ten years old again. "I know I let you down when I joined the navy and said I didn't want to be a rancher."

"No, you did not." Dad laid a calloused hand on his shoulder and Matt feared he might fall apart completely. "God gave you a different calling, just like your brothers. I understand that." His father let go then and shuffled toward the fireplace, his worn hat still clutched in his hand. "It was me. I let myself down. Not to mention your mama."

Matt couldn't believe what he was hearing.

Dad had never talked like this before. "How can you say that? As far as Mama was concerned, you hung the moon."

The old man sniffed. "If I'd have just taken better care of her..." His voice cracked. "Insisted she go to the doctor sooner..."

He moved alongside his father. "Dad, we all know she wouldn't have listened. She was too busy taking care of all of us."

Dad looked at him, his smile tremulous as a tear trailed down his cheek. "That's because she did it so well."

Matt couldn't help himself. He put an arm around his father's shoulders. "Yes, she did. And we were blessed to have her."

The old man turned into his embrace and hugged him. "I love you, son."

"I love you, too, Dad."

There in front of the Christmas tree, they held on to each other as years of misunderstandings melted away. Something Matt never would have dreamed possible. Yet, by the grace of God, here they stood.

He was curious, though.

Releasing his father, he said, "What prompted you to come here today to tell me all of this?"

Dad wiped his eyes. "Hillary."

"Did she force you?"

"Son, you know me better than that."

True. No one was going to make Clint Stephens do anything he didn't want to do.

"She's a good listener. She suggested I swallow my pride and make amends with you before it was too late."

"Suggested, huh?"

Dad looked a little sheepish. "I do love you, Matt. Always have, always will."

"Same here, Dad."

The old man scratched a hand through his thick hair. "What do you say we go grab some dinner over at Granny's Kitchen?"

The corners of Matt's mouth twitched. "So you can have an excuse to see Hillary?"

"What do you take me for, some teenager? If I want a good meal, Granny's Kitchen is the place to go."

Matt quirked a brow. "And the fact that Hillary will probably be there has nothing to do with it?"

"So I happen to like her. Shoot me."

He laughed. "It's all right, Dad. You're allowed to have a life." He shrugged. "Besides, I like Hillary, too. She knows how to keep you in line."

His father grinned. "Nah, she's just bossy."

Sounded like the pot calling the kettle black. "Give me a minute to change and we'll go."

Twenty minutes later, in a booth at Granny's

Kitchen, over a cup of coffee, Matt told his father about Marissa, Kenzie and the phone call Lacie received last night. "I don't know what I'm going to do if she takes that job."

"I know this is pointing out the obvious, but you are Kenzie's father. You could always sue for custody."

And make Lacie hate him? "I couldn't do that. Kenzie barely knows me."

"I understand." Dad wrapped both hands around his own white cup. "Well, a housing boom usually means a greater need for law enforcement. You could always follow them."

He eyed his father across the high-gloss wooden tabletop. "I thought about that."

"But?"

"It wouldn't be the same." He shrugged. "Here I'm able to drop by and see them even when I'm on duty. And Barbara's more than happy to help out with Kenzie, giving Lacie and me time together." He started to take a sip, then stopped. "You know, if we need to discuss something."

Now his father was the one with the curious lift to his brow. "Sounds like this isn't just about Kenzie."

He thought about Lacie's smile and amazing eyes. "Lacie is unlike any woman I've ever known. Sure, she's pretty, but there's so much more." He stared into the steaming black liquid. "I mean, she sacrificed everything to be a mother to Kenzie when Marissa died."

"That takes a special person, all right."

Turning toward the window, he took in all of the twinkling lights up and down Main Street. "She's definitely special."

"Sounds to me like you're falling in love."

His gaze jerked to his father's. "Love?" He scratched his head, hoping to dismiss what he knew in his heart to be true. "I don't know about that. Didn't you see the way we butted heads over a simple Christmas tree yesterday?"

"I saw the way you two worked together when you thought Kenzie was missing."

Dad lifted his cup. "Either way, I recommend you figure it out before it's too late."

Chapter Twelve

At The Paisley Elk Thursday afternoon, Lacie parked her laptop on the sales counter beside the cash register. Since Thursdays were usually slow, her mother had stayed home with Kenzie, allowing Lacie to hold down the fort here at the shop. And while Lacie wasn't sure just how much of a break her mother was getting, it enabled her to get in some much-needed on-line shopping without a five-year-old looking over her shoulder.

Aside from searching for gifts, she really wanted to find a Christmas outfit for Kenzie. Maybe a cute tunic with a ruffled skirt and colorful leggings or even a classic white fur and red velvet dress like Lacie and Marissa used to wear when they were kids.

She typed in the web address for a company that specialized in children's clothing. Concentrating on Christmas would also keep her from dwelling on that job in Colorado Springs. Despite calling them Tuesday and sending her resume and portfolio as they'd requested, she had yet to hear anything regarding an interview. To say she was getting impatient would be an understatement. Even if she wasn't sure how she felt about moving Kenzie to someplace entirely new. They'd basically be starting over and Kenzie had already faced more than her fair share of changes this past year.

Still, it would be nice to have their own place again. And they'd still be together. That is, unless Matt decided he wanted to keep Kenzie here and took measures to ensure that.

She shrugged off the unsavory thought. With all the fun they'd been having together lately, it was difficult to imagine him doing such a thing. Then again, the more Matt was with Kenzie the more inclined he might be to want permanent custody.

Grabbing her tote bag from the floor, she retrieved her phone and brought up the picture of the three of them in front of their Christmas tree. At times, it felt as though they were a family.

Silly. She clicked off the phone and put it away. The only thing between her and Matt was Kenzie and that's the way it would stay. Or so she kept telling herself. Yet the more time they spent together…

The bell over the door jangled and she looked up to see Valerie coming into the store.

"Hey, Valerie." She hurried around to the other side of the counter, past the ornate chalkboard artfully adorned with the words Happy Holidays and a rack of sweaters to give her fellow thespian a hug. "It's so nice to see you again." After getting to know her during the week of the play, Lacie had grown quite fond of her new friend.

"I just can't seem to stop thinking about you." The woman let go of her with a pat and admired the festive decorations. "Your mother sure knows how to decorate. This place is amazing."

"Yes, Mom is very good at doing festive." So long as it's not Christmas. "Can I help you find something?"

"Not today." Valerie smiled at her. "I just popped in to see if you were here. I have something I want to talk to you about."

"I'm all ears."

"I was having lunch with a friend in Ridgway yesterday and I overheard two gentlemen talking at the next table."

Lacie lifted a brow. "I think that's called eavesdropping, Valerie."

"Not when they're talking loud, it's not." She

winked. "Turns out, they were builders. You know, for those really expensive homes over there in Telluride. Anyway—" she waved a hand "—they are in the market for an interior designer. Someone who can work with their clients to help them choose all those decorative things that go into a home."

Though she was definitely intrigued about the job opportunity, she curiously eyed her friend. "You *overheard* all of this?"

"I may have asked them a few questions." Adjusting the purse strap over her shoulder, Valerie blushed. "And when I told them that I knew someone who'd been working in Denver, but was looking for something out here on the Western Slope, they gave me their card—" she pulled it from her pocket and held it out "—and said they'd love to hear from you."

Lacie took hold of the card, feeling rather stupefied. "You did all of that for me?"

"I told you we'd love to keep you here."

Her heart melted into a puddle right there. "Valerie, that is the sweetest thing anyone has ever done for me." She again hugged the woman, wondering what God might be up to. First the news about Colorado Springs, now this. "Thank you."

The always chipper brunette set Lacie away

from her and gave her one of those motherly looks. "Does that mean you're going to call them?"

Lacie met her gaze. "Yes, ma'am, I will definitely call them."

"Oh, good, because I plan to keep on praying they'll hire you."

The door jangled again, ushering in a blast of chilly air as both women turned.

This time, Matt walked in, dressed in his uniform, removing his aviator sunglasses, just as he had that first day Lacie arrived in Ouray. "Afternoon, ladies."

"Hi, Matt." Valerie turned back to Lacie. "You let me know what they say, okay?"

"I will."

Valerie smiled. "Gotta run." She waved. "See you later."

Matt paused beside the chalkboard as the door closed. "What was that all about?"

Lacie chuckled, returning to her computer. "Valerie was telling me about a design job she heard about in Telluride."

Matt followed her. "I like the sound of that." His dark gaze fixed on Lacie, he leaned his elbows against the opposite side of the counter.

For a moment, the hope she saw in his eyes took hold of her. Then she reminded herself it was only about keeping Kenzie close by.

"If you're looking for Kenzie, she's at home with Mom."

"I know. I stopped by there first. I'm here to see you."

Her traitorous heart leaped.

"You know how I told you that Dad and I made amends?"

"How could I forget?" He'd come straight to her house after having dinner with the man, bubbling over with joy as he told her all that had transpired. The news had brought happy tears to her eyes.

"Well, he called me this morning and asked if we would come out to the ranch on Sunday so everyone could meet Kenzie."

So he did only want to see her about Kenzie. "But we haven't told Kenzie that you're her father."

"I know. And I don't intend to tell her any time soon. They're aware of that." He fingered a bar of specialty chocolate displayed on the counter. "But it's never too early to start building relationships with family."

Family. Something she seemed to be losing more of all the time. And if Matt decided to take Kenzie—

She shook her head, disgusted by her self-pity. She couldn't keep Kenzie from knowing

Matt or his family. That little girl deserved all the love she could get.

Stiffening her spine, she said, "What time would you like to pick her up?"

Matt straightened, looking confused. "Pick her up? Lacie, I said *we*. That means you, me and Kenzie."

"Oh. I just thought—"

He reached across the counter and took hold of her hand. "I wouldn't exclude you. We're a team."

A team. As in one for all and all for one. Kenzie being that one. Except the gleam in Matt's eye spoke of other things. Things that had her believing that staying in Ouray might not be so bad after all.

"Now, this is the Gladys we're all used to seeing." Her blue eyes were bright, her color was good, her spirits were up as Matt would have expected. And even though she was perfectly capable of doing it herself, he added another couple of logs to the wood-burning stove Friday morning.

This was the first time he'd visited his former schoolteacher since she came home from the hospital two weeks ago, but then, with so many others checking on her and bringing her food, he didn't want to wear her out.

"I do have a confession, Matt." Gladys set the cup of coffee he'd made for her on the table beside her recliner. "I was none too pleased with you when they loaded me into that ambulance."

After closing the doors on the stove, he crossed the beige carpet to kneel beside her. "I know. I wasn't too pleased about it, either, but I had to exercise some tough love. You needed the extra care."

Smiling, she patted his hand with her wrinkled one. "And you knew just what you were doing. If I'd have stayed here, I probably would have been dead in days."

While he may have known it to be true, he wasn't ready to acknowledge it. "So what can I do for you today?"

She wrinkled her nose. "Nothing. I'm doing just fine, thanks to you."

"Aw, come on, Gladys." He gently nudged her arm. "There's got to be something you're craving. Help me out and tell me what that is."

She stared out the window for a moment, watching the snow fall to the ground. "Well, I don't expect you to do it now, but I've found myself with a hankering for some of those cinnamon rolls from the Miner's Café. Maybe you could pick me up a few the next time you're in there."

He smiled, knowing he wouldn't wait. "That

would be Granny's Kitchen. Remember, Mrs. Ward's granddaughter, Celeste, now owns it."

She wagged a finger. "That's right."

"But she uses her grandmother's recipe."

The older woman perched her clasped hands over her smaller-than-usual belly. "Yes, those are some mighty fine cinnamon rolls."

"They are, indeed." He stood. "Matter of fact, I'm kind of craving one myself. What do you say I go pick us up a pan?"

Gladys looked like she'd just stolen the last cookie from the cookie jar. "Can you do that?"

"Young lady, I have sworn to serve and protect. And I am here to serve you."

The woman snickered into her hand.

"I'll be back in a jiffy." Amid the falling snow, he hurried outside to his Tahoe. Oh, how he loved that woman. And was glad to see her back to her old self.

He pulled out of her drive and, a few minutes later, eased into a parking space near Granny's Kitchen with a smile on his face and a song in his heart. Something that seemed to happen a lot more often lately. Between learning that he had a daughter and a restored relationship with his father, life was sweeter than it had been in a long time. Now if only Lacie would decide to stay in Ouray.

He didn't know what he'd do if she took that

job in Colorado Springs. Probably follow them. Because the thought of living without her and Kenzie was more than he could bear.

Thanks to Valerie, though, Colorado Springs might not even be a blip on Lacie's radar anymore. He could only pray that job in Telluride would come through.

Opening the door of his vehicle, he stepped out into the crisp late-morning air and continued onto the sidewalk.

"Morning, Matt." Kaleb Palmer, a wounded warrior and Ouray's most decorated hero who was now owner of Mountain View Jeep Tours, looked a little weary.

"Hey, Kaleb." He shook his old schoolmate's hand. "You doin' all right? You don't look so good."

Kaleb rubbed the back of his neck. "Ah, the twins are teething, so Grace and I had kind of a rough night."

"Yeah, from what I hear teething is tough enough with one, but you've got double trouble."

The corners of Kaleb's mouth lifted. "We wouldn't trade it for the world, though. Will and Whitney have brought so much joy into our lives."

"I hear ya." Just the thought of Kenzie could brighten his spirits. "Hang in there and tell

Grace I said merry Christmas." He clapped his friend on the shoulder before he walked away.

"Will do, buddy."

At the corner, Matt reached for the restaurant's door handle.

"Matt!"

Kenzie?

Turning in the direction of Main Street, he saw her happily running across the street all by herself as though she didn't have a care in the world—and a truck moving rapidly toward her.

His gaze jerked from her to the driver. She'd bolted so fast and was so small he knew the driver couldn't see her.

"Kenzie!" Lacie stood frozen on the opposite corner, watching the horror unfold.

His heart jackhammered against his tactical vest. He had to get to his little girl before that truck got to her.

Though adrenaline pushed him forward, his legs felt like lead as he rushed into the wet street.

All around him, everything seemed to be moving in slow motion. Him, Kenzie… Everything except for that truck.

He waved his arms wildly, desperately trying to get the driver's attention.

People on the sidewalks yelled for the man to stop. But he didn't.

All the while, a grinning Kenzie kept moving toward Matt, oblivious to the danger headed straight for her.

God, I need Your help! Please don't let my daughter die!

A guttural sound he didn't even recognize escaped his throat as he made a final lunge toward Kenzie.

His arm made contact.

He scooped her up and dove out of the way as the truck skidded to a halt.

Clutching his daughter to his chest, he sat in the middle of the street, trying to catch his breath. *Thank You, God. Thank You.*

The panicked driver exited the vehicle. "I'm so sorry! I didn't see her."

Matt sucked in a large amount of bone-chilling air and held up a reassuring hand. "I know. You're fine. Just move on." He was too spent to worry about anything besides his little girl.

Those who had been looking on began to clap as Matt stood and continued across the street with Kenzie still in his arms. He didn't care about their applause, though. The simple fact that she was safe was all that mattered.

Pressing his face into her jacket, he willed his emotions to remain at bay. Not only did Kenzie need him, Lacie did, too. And just as God was there for him, he would be there for them.

The flow of traffic had resumed by the time he reached the corner. A frantic Lacie took Kenzie from him and hugged her tight.

"Thank God, you're all right." Her watery eyes found his. "I don't know what happened. I was holding her hand. She took off so fast…" After a final squeeze, she set Kenzie to the ground.

The child who had been unaware of what was going on only a few seconds ago now pooched out her bottom lip as she slowly looked up at him, tears welling in her big brown eyes. "But I wanted to see you."

His heart nearly broke.

He knelt beside her and took hold of her tiny hand. "I want to see you, too, Kenzie. But you're too small to be crossing the street by yourself." The mere thought of what could have happened clogged his throat.

He swallowed hard. "Promise me that next time you will tell your aunt Lacie and wait for her to cross the street with you."

"I promise."

When he glanced up at Lacie, he noticed that all of the color had drained from her face.

Uh-oh.

He shot to his feet. "Lace, you okay?"

She started to sway. Her eyes rolled.

Lifting her into his arms, he said, "Kenzie,

you stay right with me." He moved to a nearby bench and watched as she climbed onto it before he sat down, still holding on to Lacie. "Lace, can you hear me?"

Her head bobbed, sending her caramel waves spilling over her shoulders. "Yeah. I guess I just lost my breath for minute."

He eased Lacie between him and Kenzie. "I think we both did."

She wrapped her arms around the child and held her close, tears streaming down her cheeks, which were slowly regaining their color. "Thank you, Matt." She straightened to look at him. "If you hadn't been there—"

He touched her cheek and brushed her tears away. "But I was. No thanks necessary." He pushed the hair away from her face. "I've got your back, Lace."

She turned away then, but not before he realized just how much he meant what he'd said. He wanted to be there for her. To have her in his life. Her and Kenzie.

His dad was right. He was in love with Lacie.

Chapter Thirteen

Lacie had never been more frightened in her entire life. Yet Matt had been there to not only save the day, but to help guide her through the aftermath. Just like he'd been there for her countless other times since she came back to Ouray.

So when he suggested they attend church together on Sunday, she found it difficult to say no. Because, after what had happened in the middle of Main Street Friday, they shared a mutual understanding of just how much they had to be grateful for.

Sitting with Matt's father and three of his brothers, however, gave her pause. Wasn't it enough that they were going to be with them at the ranch later this afternoon? It wasn't that she didn't like them, it was just so…familial. And she wasn't quite prepared for that.

Nonetheless, she supposed she'd better get used to it. After all, that was the whole reason they were going to the ranch. Kenzie was a Stephens, meaning Lacie would likely be seeing all of them a lot.

When the service ended, she and Matt picked up Kenzie from her class and made their way to his Jeep through a fresh layer of snow.

"I love singing those old Christmas carols." Lacie opened the passenger-side door. "There's something about them that's very comforting."

"I couldn't agree more." Matt carried Kenzie, who insisted on wearing her red patent leather Mary Janes despite the decent amount of snow that had fallen overnight and continued coming down. "It's that sense of tradition, not to mention the true meaning of Christmas within their words, that makes them special."

He hooked Kenzie into her booster seat, which they'd transferred from Lacie's SUV, before sliding into the driver's seat. "Shall we grab some lunch?" Then, since they had yet to say anything to Kenzie, he mouthed the words, *before we head to the ranch.*

"I suppose that would be all right." Lacie adjusted her scarf. "I could go for a hot bowl of stew." Even though it meant they'd be together the entire day. Something that seemed to be happening a lot more often.

"No!" Kenzie pouted in the back seat. "I want to go home."

Lacie twisted to face her. "You don't want to get some chicken nuggets?"

"No." Arms crossed over her chest, Kenzie adamantly shook her head. "I want to see Grandma." Strange, since she usually loved to go out.

Lacie glanced at Matt. "I'm not sure what's gotten into her."

He put the vehicle into gear. "No point in making her go."

She shrugged and faced forward again, debating her next move. But since they'd already agreed to lunch… "I can make up some soup and sandwiches at home. If you're interested."

He eyed her across the center console. "I'm a bachelor, Lace. I'm always interested in food. Especially the home-cooked variety."

When they arrived at her mother's, Lacie unhooked Kenzie. "You want me to carry you so your feet won't get wet?"

Without responding, the determined child scooted past her and ran right through the snow to the house.

A grinning Matt came alongside her as they followed. "I guess you have your answer."

Lacie shook her head. "She sure is acting weird." Yet she couldn't imagine why.

"I wouldn't worry about it." He leaned closer. "She's going to have a great time once we get to the ranch."

She bent in his direction. "True, but we'd still better keep that to ourselves until after lunch. Otherwise, we'll never get her to eat."

Kenzie let herself in and by the time Matt and Lacie made it inside, she was already in the kitchen.

"How was church?" Mom stood at the island, tossing a salad.

"We learneded about baby Jesus." Still wearing her coat with the mittens dangling from the sleeves, Kenzie crawled up onto one of the stools that lined one side of the island.

Lacie closed the door, but waited in the living room, curious as to what her niece was up to.

"You did?" Mom tried to act engaged.

"Uh-huh," Kenzie continued, more animated than usual. "'Cept He didn't stay a baby. He growed up."

"He did?" Mom looked a little wary, her curious gaze shifting from Kenzie to Lacie and Matt as they approached the sofa.

"And guess what?" Kenzie's brown eyes were wide, as was her grin. She was in rare form today.

"What?" Mom tried to mimic her granddaughter's excitement, but failed.

"He loves us *this* much." Kenzie stretched her arms as wide as they would go, her mittens swaying to and fro.

Mom didn't respond, though. She simply focused on her salad. The thing should be good and tossed by now.

Seemingly annoyed, Kenzie climbed onto the counter. She was not about to be ignored. Evidently, she had something to say and she was going to say it.

"Young lady—" Mom looked horrified "—you know better than to—"

Undeterred, Kenzie plopped down on her knees in front of her grandmother, laid a hand on either side of the woman's face and forced her to look at her.

Lacie had to put a hand over her mouth to keep from laughing. Glancing over at Matt, she noticed that he was every bit as humored about what was going on as she was.

Nose inches away from her grandmother, Kenzie said, "And He loves you, too, Grandma."

Lacie's mouth fell open now. If she hadn't been here to witness this… But, boy, was she glad she was. She laid a hand to her chest as tears pricked the backs of her eyes. *And a child shall lead them.*

Turning, she started for the hallway before she cried in earnest.

Matt followed her.

She pulled a tissue from her pocket and dabbed her eyes. "I don't think I've ever been prouder of that little girl. Who knew she could preach like that?"

"No kidding." He smiled. "Though I'm pretty proud of you, too," he whispered.

She peered up at him. "Why?"

"All these years, you were the one who saw to it Kenzie was in church. You helped instill those convictions in her and I, for one, really appreciate that."

Lacie gave a tremulous smile, her heart feeling as though it had been set beside an enormous bonfire. "And if Kenzie's words happen to impact Mom, then even better."

After changing into clothes more appropriate for the ranch, Lacie returned to the kitchen to start on lunch. Now that Kenzie had accomplished what she'd set out to do when they left church, she was more interested in playing with Matt. So Lacie decided to wait until *after* they told her they were going to the ranch to talk her niece into changing. A little motivation never hurt to keep things running smoothly.

She grabbed a can of tomato soup from the cupboard and cheese and butter from the fridge. All the while she could feel her mother watching her from the table as she slowly chewed her salad.

Really? Who had a salad on a cold day like this?

She dared a glance across the island.

Her mother, that was who.

Oh, well. To each her own. Lacie had too many other things to think about besides what her mother thought of Kenzie's little sermon. Like the two job prospects she had looming out there.

After putting the soup on to heat, she readied a skillet and opened the loaf of bread. She'd contacted the gentleman in Telluride, who'd seemed very interested, and sent him her resume. He'd promised to get back in touch with her tomorrow.

In addition, she'd finally heard back from the company in Colorado Springs and had a phone interview scheduled with them for tomorrow afternoon. This was shaping up to be a busy week.

Yet, as she buttered the first slice of bread, she couldn't decide which job she'd prefer more. While staying in Ouray would be nice, there were so many more opportunities in the eastern part of the state. Then again, back there it'd be just her and Kenzie. Here, they'd have all kinds of friends and family. People who could help out, should the need arise.

Lord, show me what You would have me do. Lead me on Your path.

Mom brought her empty bowl to the sink as Lacie laid the first sandwich in the pan. The butter sizzled when it made contact with the heat, much like the feel of her mother's gaze boring into her. It was only a matter of time before—

"So did you put Kenzie up to that?"

Spatula in hand, she faced her mother. "You know, Mom, I wish I could say I did." She couldn't help smiling. "But, like it or not, that was all Kenzie."

To her surprise, Mom didn't respond. She merely lowered her gaze and walked away.

Matt couldn't remember the last time he'd actually looked forward to going to the ranch. Sure there'd been a few times since his mother died that his presence had been requested and he'd forced himself to go, but his visits were always overshadowed by an enormous sense of dread at the thought of seeing his father.

All these years, he'd never imagined his father had been hurting, too. That he'd wanted to reconcile, but had been just as afraid as Matt to make a move. And while Matt had feared the news about Kenzie would have deepened the chasm between them, it had instead brought healing and allowed them to start anew.

Thank You, God, for redeeming something I thought unsalvageable.

Now, as they headed toward the ranch, he could hardly wait to introduce his daughter to everything it had to offer. Fishing, exploring, climbing trees, riding horses and so much more. Not that they'd be able to do many of those things today, but now that the snow had stopped, they might get in something fun.

"Are we there yet?" Kenzie wiggled in her booster seat.

"Almost." In the passenger seat of his Jeep, Lacie rolled her pretty eyes. "Imagine hearing that question over and over for five hours."

He shuddered. That alone should be incentive enough for her *not* to take the job back east, should they offer it to her. That and the fact that he didn't want her to go. Because the more time he spent with her, the more he realized just how special she was.

"Horsies!" Kenzie said as they approached the ranch.

He peered at her via the rearview mirror. "Hey, how would you like to ride one of those horses, Kenzie?"

Her arms shot straight into the air. "Yay!"

"Wh—" Lacie's head jerked in his direction. "You're not serious about that, are you?"

"Sure, why not?" He sent her a curious glance

as they turned into the drive and continued under the arched sign. "I was a lot younger than her the first time I sat on a horse."

"Yeah, but you were around them your entire life. Until Monday, Kenzie had never even seen one up close." Why was she getting so worked up?

"Lacie, it's all right. You know I wouldn't do anything to put her in danger."

Her expression was incredulous. "Oh, you mean like you did Marissa."

"What?"

"You know, the time you took her horseback riding and the horse bolted into the woods." She shook her head. "Her neck was scraped and scratched from one side to the other from being dragged through the trees."

Oops. He'd forgotten about that. "I blame Noah for that. He promised that horse was perfect for a novice."

She cast a wary glance at the stable as they passed. "And that's supposed to make me feel better?"

"I'll be choosing the horse this time." Not to mention that he and his brother were both a lot wiser now.

"It's not you I'm worried about. It's an unpredictable animal."

They bumped the rest of the way up the long

drive in silence. He couldn't help wondering if what had happened on Friday was playing a part in Lacie's sudden overprotectiveness. Because when they'd taken Kenzie to see the horses last Monday, Lacie had been fine.

"Pretty lights," said Kenzie when they pulled up to the ranch house. Obviously the heated exchange between him and Lacie hadn't affected her.

He eyed the colorful strands of lights that now adorned the railing of the deck and smiled. Evidently the grouchy old coot they'd run into at the supercenter last week had found his Christmas spirit. And perhaps it had something to do with the little girl in the back seat.

Emerging from his vehicle, he noticed Andrew's truck parked on the other side of their father's dually.

"Looks like Andrew and Carly are already here." Considering Noah, Jude and Daniel lived at the ranch, it looked like he, Lacie and Kenzie were the last to arrive.

He helped Kenzie from the back seat and held her hand as the three of them made their way onto the long deck. Fresh snow crunched under their boots, yet despite the gray clouds overhead, he couldn't help feeling that this was going to be a good day.

When they entered the ranch house, the first

thing Matt smelled was pine, reminding him of Christmases from long ago. His heart warmed. Deciding to cut down a real tree had been the right thing to do. In this house, nothing else would do.

After removing their boots in the mudroom, they continued into the family room with its wood-burning stove and overstuffed yet oh-so-comfortable furniture. And there in front of the picture window was the tree. Smaller than he was used to seeing, but magnificent nonetheless.

"There they are." A grinning Dad set his coffee cup on the off-white counter and started toward them from the adjoining kitchen. Stopping, he looked straight at Matt. "Glad you could make it, son."

A lump formed in Matt's throat. It had been a long time since he'd felt welcomed in this house.

He did his best to shake off the emotion. "I wouldn't have missed it, Dad."

"Lacie, good to see you again." The old man patted her on the arm.

"Thank you for inviting us," she said.

Lowering his gaze, Dad smiled at his granddaughter. "And how are you today, Miss Kenzie?"

"Good." She leaned into Lacie. Something Matt had come to expect whenever his daughter was feeling shy or insecure.

Hillary approached then. "Hello, everyone."

Carly followed and hugged Lacie. "I'm so glad you're here." His sister-in-law then knelt in front of Kenzie. "Megan's been looking forward to seeing you again."

His daughter straightened and smiled, obviously feeling more confident. "Where is she?"

Carly stood. "She and Andrew are at the stables." She looked at him now. "Noah is giving her a riding lesson."

Kenzie gasped, her face beaming. "I want to ride the horsies, too."

"I'm sure we can arrange that." Hands resting on his denim-clad hips, Dad continued to watch the little girl.

Recalling their conversation in the Jeep, Matt glanced at Lacie.

Her eyes were wide as she looked at Carly. "Lessons, huh?"

"Oh, yes. Megan loves horses, so the more knowledge she has about them, the safer she'll be."

He'd have to remember to thank his sister-in-law later.

"You think we have a helmet small enough for Kenzie?" He eyed his father, hoping that the mention of safety equipment would help put Lacie at ease.

"Sure. We got all sizes."

He figured as much, considering Abundant Blessings Ranch not only offered lessons but trail rides during the summer months. Something Noah had been working toward expanding into a full-blown rodeo school.

"Can we go now?" While Lacie might be nervous, Kenzie was more than ready.

Dad looked from his granddaughter to Matt then Lacie. "I don't know why not."

"But she's only five." Lacie fiddled with the zipper on her coat. She still wasn't sold.

"Ah, she'll do just fine," said Dad. "You can even go down there with her."

"C'mon, Aunt Lacie." Kenzie tugged on her arm. "Let's go."

Still looking none too certain, Lacie reluctantly followed Kenzie across the wood laminate flooring toward the mudroom.

Matt fell in beside her, determined to put her at ease. "Don't worry, Lace. I'll be with her the whole time."

However, the glare she sent him said he hadn't reassured her at all.

Chapter Fourteen

Lacie had a bad feeling about this.

Following Matt and a helmeted Kenzie down a long aisle lined with stalls, she drew in a shaky breath, the smell of hay and horse filling her nostrils.

"My brother Noah helped me choose the perfect horse for you." Matt smiled down at Kenzie.

"What's its name?" She tilted her little face to look at him.

"His name is Toby."

"He's a boy?"

Matt chuckled. "That's usually how it works."

He was putting her on a male horse?

Passing another stall, Lacie eyed the big fellow Matt had introduced them to last week. The one he said was Noah's horse. The dark brown creature was huge.

Gentle or not, why would Matt risk putting a little girl on something so massive?

She double stepped to catch up with them. "I'm sorry, Matt. I just don't think this is a good—"

"Here we go, Kenzie." As though ignoring Lacie, Matt stopped in front of one of the stalls and slid the wood-and-metal door to one side. "Meet Toby." His gaze shifting to Lacie, he motioned for her to have a look.

"Oh…" Hands clasped against her chest, Kenzie eyed the animal with wonder.

Taking a step closer, Lacie peered inside to see a small black-and-white horse. "A pony?" Young and barely trained. She sent Matt a questioning gaze.

He continued into the stall. "A Shetland pony." He rubbed a hand over the animal. "He's eight years old." He sent Lacie a pointed stare. "We keep him especially for kids."

Suddenly embarrassed, she backed off while he bridled and saddled the horse. She shouldn't have doubted him. She'd seen how he responded when Kenzie flew into the street two days ago. He'd put his own life on the line to save her. So why did she think he wouldn't have Kenzie's best interests at heart now?

Still, animals were unpredictable. What if something spooked the horse or it didn't want to be ridden? She closed her eyes. After what happened Friday, she was more afraid than ever.

Matt led Toby into the aisle. "We're ready to go."

Lacie fell in beside Kenzie. "You listen to everything Matt tells you and do exactly what he says."

"Okay."

While Matt continued into the small indoor arena with Kenzie and Toby, Lacie joined Clint, Noah, Andrew and Megan at the railing.

"She'll be just fine." Clint winked.

Matt lifted Kenzie into the saddle and got her situated.

"Aunt Lacie, look at me."

Lacie couldn't help but smile. She pulled out her phone and opened the camera.

"Smile." She snapped a couple of shots.

Matt led the animal and Kenzie around the large circle.

Kenzie's smile had never been bigger, though she also seemed to understand the importance of paying attention to what she was doing.

"That a girl," said Clint.

Kenzie waved as they passed and Lacie caught another picture.

While Noah, Andrew and Megan discussed her lesson, Lacie turned to Clint.

"Thank you for being so good to Kenzie, welcoming her like this."

He perched a boot on one of the fence rungs. "You and Kenzie are welcome here anytime."

She nodded uncomfortably, knowing what she still needed to say. "I also want to apologize for my sister's actions. Keeping Kenzie away from all of you, not letting Matt know…"

The older man's smile was one of understanding. "It doesn't matter how she got here—she's here now. And we couldn't be more pleased."

She again searched out Kenzie. Something wasn't right, though. "Is it my imagination or is she leaning?" And with every step the horse took, the saddle and Kenzie inched farther down Toby's side.

"Saddle isn't cinched," said Clint.

Matt looked at Kenzie then, but it was too late.

Kenzie toppled off the horse.

"No!" Lacie climbed the rungs, thrust herself over the railing and rushed toward Kenzie. What if the horse stepped on her? He may be small, but he still weighed a lot more than a little girl.

She reached them as Matt lifted Kenzie to her feet.

"You okay, small fry?"

How could he take this so lightly? It wasn't as though she'd simply stumbled.

Then she heard it. Kenzie was—laughing?

Looking up at Matt, she dusted herself off. "That was fun."

Fun? She was practically having a heart attack and Kenzie thought it was fun?

Matt barely glanced at Lacie before turning his attention back to his daughter. "Let's get this saddle tightened up so you can ride some more."

Feeling like a fool for overreacting, she made her way across the arena.

Clint opened the gate for her. "Looks like we might need to get you on a horse, too."

She faced him as he closed it, only to see a mischievous grin. "I'm sorry. I don't usually overreact like that."

He set a calloused hand on her shoulder. "I guess you're still pretty rattled about what happened Friday."

"That obvious, huh?"

"Just a little." He held up a finger and thumb. "If there's one thing I've learned raising five boys, it's that no matter how good of a parent you are, they're still going to get hurt, they're going to get sick, they're gonna cry and they're going to do some of the *stupidest* things you can imagine."

She laughed then.

His weathered expression turned more serious. "The only thing we can do is love them." His dark eyes so reminiscent of Matt's drifted toward the arena. "And sometimes we don't even get that right." He cleared his throat. "What I'm trying to say is that you're a fine mama to that little girl and, even though he's new to it, I think Matt's going to be a great dad."

Looking over her shoulder, she watched Matt put Kenzie back into the saddle. "I think he already is."

When the ride was over, Kenzie went on back to the house with Clint, Noah, Andrew and Megan while Lacie helped Matt put things away at the stables. He was unusually quiet, though, and she had a pretty good idea why.

"I'm sorry I overreacted." Standing in the doorway of the tack room, hands shoved in the pockets of her puffer, she watched as he put things away.

"Nah, I get it." He hung up the bridle, never even looking her way. "You're still freaked out from the other day."

"That's true, I am. But I don't want you to think that I don't trust you. I mean, after all, you were the one who saved her. I just stood there like a bump on a log." If he hadn't been there, Kenzie could have been killed while she watched.

He stopped what he was doing and finally

faced her. "Is that what this is all about?" He moved toward her then. "Are you blaming yourself for what happened?"

All of the emotions she'd been holding in rose to the surface. Her throat thickened. Her bottom lip began to quiver.

She quickly turned away. "I couldn't stop her." Looking toward the rafters, she blinked several times. "One second I had a hold of her hand and the next—" A sob caught in her throat. Her body began to shake.

"Look at me, Lace."

She didn't want to, but he stepped in front of her and made her do it anyway.

"Aw, Lace." He took her into his arms and that was it. Everything she'd been fighting so hard to keep inside let loose. All of the pent-up angst, disappointment and failure flooded to the surface.

"It's all my fault," she cried. "I should have stopped her, but I didn't."

He tightened his hold. "It's all right. We never know how we're going to react when we're put in situations like that."

"No, it's not all right." Her anger spilled out. Breaking free, she moved into the tack room. "Nothing is all right. I lost my job. I'm the reason we don't have a home. The reason Kenzie isn't going to be able to wake up Christmas morning and walk down the hall in her own house to a tree filled with presents and Christmas music playing in the background. It's all because of me." Exhausted, she dropped onto a bale of hay, covered her face with her hands and, for the first time since she became Kenzie's guardian, she let her tears fall freely.

When she finally stopped, she lifted her head to see Matt kneeling in front of her with a roll of paper towels.

"Not as soft as tissues," he said, "but at least they're absorbent."

Smiling, she pulled off a few sheets and blotted her face. "I'm sorry you had to see that." He probably thought her a lunatic.

"I'm not. Now I know you're human."

She peered up at him. "As opposed to…?"

"Well, we won't go there." Grinning, he tugged her to her feet, but didn't let go of her hands. "You know, a dam can only hold so much before it breaks. Sounds like you've been holding in an awful lot."

She nodded, her cheeks growing warm.

"You're not alone, Lacie. I know you think you need to do and take care of everything yourself, but there are plenty of us who want to help you. Me, your mom…me."

"I know." Seemed he'd proved that over and

over, clear back to that day he helped her with her battery.

He glanced toward the window. "I hate to bring this up, but we should probably head on up to the house for dinner."

She groaned, covering her face. "I must look a mess."

"Not at all." Pulling her hand away, he touched her cheek. "You look beautiful."

"Yeah, right."

"I mean it, Lace. You're the most beautiful woman I've ever known." He looked so serious.

Her insides tangled. But she knew better than to allow herself to be sucked in.

She turned for the door. "They're waiting on us."

Matt finished clearing off the worn-out wooden dining room table that had been left behind by the previous owners when he bought his house. The scarred and scratched surface may not be pretty, but it was flat, making it the perfect spot for wrapping presents.

He retrieved the few gifts he'd already bought for Kenzie, along with scissors and tape. Now he just needed Lacie to get here with the wrapping paper and her presents. Since Barbara had agreed to keep Kenzie, they'd decided this would be a good time to compare each of their gift selections so they could see what else they might need, as well as wrap without fear of Kenzie walking in on them.

Returning to the living room, he turned on some Christmas music and cleared the crumbs littering the coffee table, his gaze drifting from the tree glowing in the corner to the empty fireplace. Something was missing, though he had yet to figure out what that something was. Perhaps it was just the lack of a fire. He'd have to make a point to swing by the ranch to pick up some wood.

A knock sounded at the door.

He opened it to find Lacie holding a large box that obscured her face and plastic bags dangling from both arms, one with two rolls of wrapping paper sticking out.

"A little help, please." She grunted.

He tossed the crumbs out the door and grabbed hold of the box. "I got it." He waited for her to enter then closed the door. "You can put the stuff in the dining room."

She made her way into the space adjacent the living room and dropped the bags into one of four peeling chairs. "Phew! That wasn't quite as easy as I thought it was going to be."

He set the box on the table. "You could have asked for help, you know. Or have you forgotten our conversation yesterday?"

Making a face, she tossed her head back. "Don't remind me. I still can't believe I did that to you."

"Uh, just what was it you did to me?"

"As if you don't remember." Casting an annoyed eye his way, she shrugged out of her puffer. "Having a meltdown is one thing. Doing it in front of someone else is just wrong."

"Not if that someone else doesn't mind." Actually, he kind of liked that she felt comfortable enough with him to let her feelings out. Made him feel as though she finally trusted him.

Now, however, he'd better change the subject. "Can I get you anything? Water, coffee, hot chocolate—it's instant."

"Yeah, I think some hot chocolate would be nice."

At least he got her to smile. "Marshmallows?"

"Of course."

Since he already had the water hot on the stove, suspecting that's what she'd go for, he quickly scooped the powder into a couple of mugs, then added the water and a spoon before grabbing the bag of marshmallows and rejoining her.

He set the items on the table. "I forgot to ask you. How did the interview go?" Today was her phone interview with the company in Colorado Springs. And while he didn't want her to fail, he wouldn't be disappointed if they chose someone else, either.

"It went well." She opened the bag, tossed a handful of marshmallows into one of the cups and stirred. "They said they liked my designs, that my style would work well with their projects..." She shrugged. "I guess I'll find out in a few days." Lifting the cup, she blew on the steaming mixture. "Oh, and I heard from the company in Telluride."

Cradling his mug, he did his best to keep his excitement under wraps. "And?"

"I have an interview with them tomorrow morning." She started to take a sip, then stopped. "In person, of course."

"That always helps. You get a better feel for people when you can see their body language and such."

"Yeah. But I have to admit, I'm a little nervous."

"You shouldn't be. With your experience and sparkling personality, they're sure to love you."

She puffed out a laugh. "I don't know about that, but I appreciate the vote of confidence." She sipped her drink. "Mmm... I like the Christmas music, too. All Mom plays at the shop is some nonholiday instrumental stuff and then nothing at home." She let go a sigh. "It's kind of depressing. So I'm glad I'm here."

"Me, too." Though he doubted she knew just how much. "You want to show me what you got for Kenzie?"

"Yes." She returned her cup to the table and opened the flaps on the box. "I really haven't gotten her any toys yet, because I wanted to wait until I knew what you were getting her." Reaching inside, she pulled out what looked like a shoe box. "I got her a pair of riding-style boots." She lifted the lid to show him.

"Nice." Though he might be in trouble.

After depositing the boots on the table, she reached inside the larger box again. "And you'll probably love this." Smiling, she pulled out a pink cowboy hat.

"Okay." He smiled back, though he was cringing inside.

"And then I got her a stuffed animal." She showed him a fluffy black-and-white horse that kind of reminded him of Toby. "Seeing as how she's now totally in love with horses."

He drew in a deep breath, set his cup down and picked up the bag of things he'd gotten Kenzie. "Lace, you know how they say 'great minds think alike'?"

"Yeah…"

He dumped the items onto the table. "Boots, cowboy hat and a stuffed horse."

Looking at his gifts, she started to laugh.

"Oh, that is too funny." She picked up his pink cowgirl boots and her pink cowboy hat. "These will go perfectly together." After setting those aside, she grabbed the identical stuffed horses. "I'll return mine." She set it in the box as he reached for the black cowboy hat he'd bought.

"And I'll return my hat. Because she's going to be so in love with the pink hat and boots that we may never get her to wear anything else."

"Oh, you're right about that." Hand on her hip, she eyed the three items they were going to give Kenzie. "You know what this means, don't you?"

"Yeah. We have a lot more shopping to do."

"And very little to wrap."

They looked at each other and laughed.

"What's in the other bags?" He pointed to the chair.

"I almost forgot." Taking hold of the first one, she reached inside. "I realized that we didn't have any stockings, so I bought us some, along with these cute stocking holders."

"Stocking holders?" He'd never heard of such a thing. At the ranch, they just hung theirs on a nail.

"I didn't want to mess up that pretty mantel of yours, so…" She held up a silver rectangle with a hook on one side. "They're weighted, so they sit on the mantel like this." She held it so the hook was on the bottom and there was a letter *J* on the top. "And then—" she grabbed one of three furry red-and-white stockings "—you simply hang your stocking on it."

"Clever." He studied it a moment. "Except, why the *J*?"

"Oh. There's also an *O* and a *Y*, so they spell *joy*. I thought about doing our initials, but with a *K*, *L* and *M*, I was afraid it would look like we'd simply carved out the middle of the alphabet."

"Good thinking."

Suddenly looking sheepish, she said, "I hope you don't mind, but I got one more thing to kind of round out the whole look."

"Lacie, you can do whatever you want."

From the final bag, she brought out some evergreen garland. "It's prelit, so I thought it would cast a nice light while illuminating the *J-O-Y*."

"Didn't you mention this that night before we got the tree?"

She tilted her head. "Yeah, you're right. And then we forgot all about it."

"Yeah, well, we took a little detour when we decided to cut down a tree." He picked up the stockings. "Shall we go put them up?" He nodded toward the living room.

In no time, she'd artfully arranged everything. He plugged in the lights before joining her near the couch. And when he turned to look at what she'd done, he could hardly believe his eyes.

"You're not going to believe this, Lace, but all week long I've been looking at the fireplace, knowing that something was missing. I thought it was simply a fire, but you hit the nail on the head."

"What do you mean?"

He turned to face her. "I've lived in this house for over a year now, worked to make it mine, and yet it's never really felt like home. Until now." Unable to stop himself, he caressed her cheek. "The decorations, all of the little touches you've added… Lacie, you've made it feel like a home."

Lowering his head, he kissed her. Something he'd wanted to do for a long time, but the moment had never felt right until tonight. With or without Kenzie, Lacie was the missing piece in his life.

He pulled her closer as her arms wound around his neck. She smelled like the wildflowers that covered the mountains in late July.

And he knew that this was definitely right.

Chapter Fifteen

By Tuesday afternoon, Lacie was sorely in need of a distraction. Something that would take her mind off Matt and that amazing kiss. She'd never been kissed like that before. In Matt's warm embrace, she'd felt safe, wanted...loved.

So she was more than grateful when Carly called, inviting her and Kenzie to come over to Granger House for some cookie decorating.

"Look, Aunt Lacie." Sitting at the table in Carly's kitchen, Kenzie held up her cookie creation. "I maded a Santa Claus."

Armed with a cup of chai tea, Lacie made her way across beautiful dark hardwood floor to where Kenzie and Megan sat surrounded by bowls of frosting and containers of sprinkles and colored sugars.

She eyed Kenzie's sparkling red confection. "Ooh, he looks good enough to eat."

"No." Suddenly perturbed, her niece quickly withdrew her masterpiece. "We hafta save him for Christmas."

"Oh, okay." Considering that Christmas was just under two weeks away, she doubted the treat would last that long.

"Don't worry, Kenzie." Beside her, ten-year-old Megan carefully frosted a snowman. "We have lots of cookies so you can take home a whole bunch."

"I can?" The little girl's brown eyes went wide as though she'd never imagined she'd get to decorate more than one cookie.

"Yep." Megan took a bite of the snowman, crumbs clinging to the corners of her mouth. "We even get samples."

Kenzie looked from Megan to the Santa cookie she still held in her hand. After a moment of contemplation, she bit into his red beard and grinned. "He tasteses good."

Chuckling, Lacie returned to the large marble-topped island, where her friend was transferring another batch of freshly baked sugar cookies to a cooling rack. "Thanks for inviting us, Carly. Kenzie is having a ball." And it gave her niece the opportunity to participate in some of those things Lacie used to do as a kid but her mother no longer allowed.

"Good." Carly set the now-empty baking

sheets atop the large commercial-style range. "The kids get jazzed on sugar and you and I get time to catch up. Sounds like a win-win to me." She picked up two warm Christmas tree–shaped treats and handed one to Lacie. "Cheers."

"Cheers." She took a bite, savoring the unexpected hint of nutmeg as she admired the baking-themed ornaments dangling from an evergreen swag over the window. "You have quite a knack for decorating." From the historic Victorian home's stunning front porch all the way through to the family room at the back, the house was a feast for the eyes with nods to the season everywhere you looked. Wreaths, seasonal vignettes, poinsettias…

Kenzie had been blown away by the fact that they had two Christmas trees. A lovely Victorian-themed one in the parlor of the bed-and-breakfast and a more casual one for Carly, Andrew and Megan in the family room.

"This place is absolutely gorgeous."

Laughing, Carly dusted the crumbs from her hands. "I know I go a little overboard, but I just can't help myself. I love Christmas."

"I know what you mean." Lacie's father used to say the same thing. Even Mom. They could hardly wait to get the Thanksgiving turkey put away so they could start on Christmas. Then

Daddy died and Christmas at their house hadn't been the same since.

But that didn't mean she couldn't resurrect those old traditions so Kenzie could experience them. And thanks to Matt and Carly, she was getting to do just that.

Carly poured herself another cup of tea. "How's the job search going? Did you ever hear from the place in Telluride?"

"Actually, I interviewed with them this morning." She eased onto one of the high-backed stools along the island.

"Yay!" Her friend joined her in the next seat. "That would mean you could stay in Ouray."

"Yes, it would." Something she found even more appealing after spending time with Matt last night. She still couldn't believe they'd picked out the same gifts. Or how pleased he'd been with her simple changes to the fireplace.

You've made it feel like home. Her heart thundered just thinking about the look in his eyes right before he kissed her.

She cleared her throat. "Mind if I get some more tea?"

"No, help yourself."

Lacie scurried around to the other side of the island and poured a cup. It would be silly for her to stay in Ouray just because of Matt, no matter how kind he'd been or how spine-tingling his kisses were. After all, there were no guarantees. And she refused to hang her hat on a man the way her sister had.

So why did those crazy notions of her, Matt and Kenzie as a family keep popping up?

"When will you know something?"

Returning to her seat, she said, "Hopefully by next week."

Carly shivered with excitement. "I'll be praying extra hard then."

Lacie cradled the warm cup in her hands. "You know that I also interviewed with a company in Colorado Springs."

Her friend waved her off. "I don't care about them. I want you to stay here." She sipped her tea, her expression taking on a more impish air. "And I'm sure Matt would like that, too."

If only. "I know he doesn't want Kenzie to go away, but—"

"I wasn't referring to Kenzie." Carly set her mug atop the marble surface. "I was talking about you."

"What do you mean? Matt and I are just friends." At least she assumed they were still friends.

Carly's brow arched. "Mmm-hmm. You just keep telling yourself that."

"I'm not sure what you're getting at." She eyed the two giggling girls across the room.

Kenzie appeared to have more frosting on her face than the cookies.

"I used to say the same thing about Andrew and me. And look where we are now." She held up her left hand and wiggled her ring finger.

Panic swirled in Lacie's gut. Were her feelings for Matt that obvious? And if Carly had been able to figure it out, did Matt know, too? More important, did he feel that way about her?

No, she refused to get her hopes up.

Then why did you kiss him?

Eager to change the subject, she said, "Matt said you two got married in September. I thought Andrew lived in Denver."

"He did. But after selling his business, he came back here last spring to work on his grandmother's house—" she pointed to the home next door "—not knowing that she'd left half of it to me. Next thing you know—"

Lacie's phone rang. She pulled it from her back pocket to see Matt's name on the screen. Her cheeks heated. Did he know they'd been talking about him?

She glanced at Carly. "I need to take this." Twisting out of the chair, she pressed the button and put the phone to her ear. "Hello."

"Hey, it's me."

"Yeah, hi." Her stomach did that fluttering thing.

"You aren't going to believe this, but I stopped

by your mom's shop earlier and she asked me if I would like her to watch Kenzie tomorrow night so that you and I could go shopping."

Lacie felt her eyes widen. "You're kidding." Turning her back to the girls and Carly, she took a few more steps so Kenzie wouldn't hear her. "I mean, yeah, I mentioned about the gifts, but still, we would be *Christmas* shopping and since she doesn't do Christmas…"

"I found it kind of strange myself. However, since she offered… Are you free tomorrow night?"

"Yes, of course." She turned back around. "The sooner we get this out of the way, the better I'll feel."

"Great. I'll pick you up about six then?"

"Sounds good."

"And Lace?"

Seemed her heart did a little quickstep every time he called her that. "Yeah?"

"I'll see you and Kenzie later tonight?"

She couldn't help smiling. "See you then."

Cup in hand, a grinning Carly leaned back in her chair as Lacie ended the call. "And you think you're just friends, huh?"

Matt enjoyed his time with Kenzie Tuesday night, though he couldn't seem to take his eyes off Lacie. Since that kiss, their relationship had drifted into uncharted waters. And all Matt knew was that he couldn't stop thinking about her.

Which made his shift on Wednesday seem excruciatingly long. Yet as the day progressed, there was one thing he began to understand: his life was finally coming together.

For too many years, he'd felt as though he was simply existing. Now he had a purpose. He was a father. And, after Monday night, had begun to entertain the notion of becoming a husband and having a family to call his own.

No doubt about it, he was in love with Lacie.

Now he just needed to find a way to share those thoughts with her.

However, the toy aisle of the supercenter in Montrose was not the right place.

"What about this art easel?" Lacie looked at him over her shoulder as they continued their search for Christmas gifts Wednesday night. "Or is that a disaster waiting to happen?"

Images of Kenzie armed with a paintbrush filled his head. "Hmm, good question. Perhaps we should keep looking."

While "Jingle Bell Rock" played overhead, they strolled from one aisle to the next, dodging other shoppers who were also searching for that perfect present.

"Are you okay?" He watched Lacie, noting

how her turquoise scarf deepened the blue of her eyes. "You seem kind of quiet tonight."

"Yeah, I'm fine." She pushed the cart, scanning each and every shelf. "Just worried about finding something that Kenzie will really enjoy. Not just play with Christmas morning and then be done with it."

He froze, a leaden weight suddenly bearing down on him. "Boy, you can tell this is my first Christmas as a dad. I never even thought of that. That would stink." He wanted his little girl to have something momentous.

Smiling, she patted him on the back. "Sorry, I didn't mean to stress you out. Just keep in mind that there are two of us, so I'm sure we can come up with something."

Out of the corner of his eye, he glimpsed the board games. "Hey, does she have a Candyland game? I used to love playing that." Then he spotted the bicycles. "Or what about a bike? One with training wheels and pink streamers hanging off the handlebars. She'd love that."

"Probably so." Resting her elbow on the cart, Lacie looked up at him. "But what if it's snowing Christmas day? She wouldn't be able to try it out."

"Good point. Better wait till spring for that." Another idea blazed across his brain. "However, we could get her a sled. Or maybe a toboggan.

Then we could take her to Vinegar Hill. We'd have a great time sledding with all of the other kids." He took hold of her arm. "I can see us now, zooming down the hill, noses pink from the cold, snow flying…"

She nodded. "That's not a bad idea. I do have one question, though."

"What's that?"

The corners of her pretty mouth tilted upward. "Is this sled for Kenzie or for you?"

He grinned. "Well, she is kind of little to be going all by herself."

"Okay—" she continued down the aisle "—so a sled for Dad and Kenzie."

He followed behind her, his chest puffed out ever so slightly. "I like the way you said that."

She slowed. "Said what?"

"The way you referred to me as Dad." He shrugged. "I'm looking forward to hearing Kenzie say it someday."

She stopped, her expression turning sad. "Matt—"

"No, no." He held up a hand. "It's okay, Lace." He knew what she was thinking. That he was pushing her to tell Kenzie he was her father when they'd agreed to wait until she was old enough to understand. "I was simply making a statement. Now, let's get back to shopping."

An hour and a half later they left the store

armed with a couple of board games, some Legos, a princess doll, Christmas pajamas and a promise that he would find them the perfect sled. This Christmas was going to be the best ever.

Now, as they headed south on Highway 550 in his Jeep with Christmas music playing softly on the radio, he could hardly wait to get back to his house so they could wrap the presents and place them under the tree. Kenzie would be so excited when she saw them.

If only he could decide what to get Lacie. Something heartfelt. Jewelry? Clothes, maybe?

He'd worry about those things another day. Tonight, he and Lacie were alone. And even more than wrapping the gifts, he wanted to talk about his and Lacie's future. Not about jobs or moving, but their feelings for each other and where those feelings could ultimately lead.

"I think we did pretty good, don't you?" He watched the darkened road ahead.

"I do. I'm glad we were able to get it out of the way."

He eyed his rearview mirror. "I can't wait to see Kenzie's face on Christmas morning."

The hum of the tires filled the space between them as Lacie stared out the passenger window.

Reaching across the center console, he gave her shoulder a squeeze. "You tired?"

"No, not too bad." She twisted in her seat to face him, but didn't say anything.

He glanced her way, slowing his speed as they came into the town of Ridgway. "Something wrong?"

Appearing somewhat nervous, she drew in a breath. "I heard from the company in Colorado Springs today."

His grip tightened around the steering wheel and he suddenly found it hard to breathe. "What'd they say?" His voice was tight.

"They offered me the job." The smile he saw via the dashboard lights felt like a knife between his shoulder blades.

This couldn't be happening. Not now. Not when they were growing so close. "Are you going to take it?" Regretting the anger that tinged his words, he added, "I mean, what about the job in Telluride? You haven't heard from them, have you?"

"No, not yet." She faced forward again as they passed under the stoplight. "And I'm still not a hundred percent sure about this one. However, it pays very well and there's room for advancement."

"But what about…?" *Us*, he almost said.

She looked at him. "What?"

"Nothing." He shook his head, accelerating again as they continued out of town.

Looking down at her clasped hands, she said, "How would you feel about it? If I decided to take this job?"

How would he feel? Did she even have to ask? Of course he didn't want her to leave. He couldn't believe she was even considering it.

And what about his daughter? Was Lacie planning to keep Kenzie away from him the way Marissa had?

"Lacie, I—" He stopped himself, his nostrils flaring. Arguing would do no good. She'd made up her mind. "You do what you want to do."

Nothing more was spoken. Just the fact that she was still considering taking Kenzie and heading back east said it all. Obviously what happened between them the other night meant nothing to her. So there was no point in going back to his place.

When they hit the Ouray city limits, he took her straight to her mother's.

Bringing the Jeep to a stop, he said, "Let me know what you decide."

Chapter Sixteen

Lacie stood in the cold night air and watched Matt drive away. She knew better than to get her hopes up. Yet she'd done it anyway. Matt wasn't interested in her. Only Kenzie.

Hands buried in her coat pockets, she forced one foot in front of the other, battling back tears as she continued up the front walk at her mother's. She needed to get away from Ouray. And the sooner the better.

Yes, she was in love with Matt, something she could kick herself for, but she'd obviously misread his feelings for her. Otherwise he would have told her not to take the job in Colorado Springs. Instead, he would have asked her to stay.

But he didn't. Leaving her free to do whatever she wanted. So why was she so torn?

She glanced toward the house. The blinds

were closed, yet she could see the glow of light beyond them. It was almost nine o'clock, so Kenzie would likely be in bed. Just as well. Lacie wasn't sure she had the strength to pretend that all was well in her world. Facing her mother was going to be tough enough.

Pausing on the porch, she slumped against the wall. *God, my heart is hurting and I don't know what to do. Should I go ahead and accept this job that will take me and Kenzie away from Ouray and Matt? Or should I wait to see what Telluride has to say?*

A chilling breeze sifted through the trees.

Staying here would mean seeing Matt on an almost daily basis. Was she prepared to deal with that?

She squeezed her eyes shut. *My heart is telling me to go, but I want to be in Your will, Lord. Show me what I should do.*

Wiping a tear from her cheek, she took a deep breath, pushed the door open and stepped inside.

"Surprise!" An overly excited Kenzie rushed toward her and took hold of her hand. "Look what we did, Aunt Lacie." She swept her little arm through the air, as if to say *tah-dah*.

Turning, a lump caught in Lacie's throat. There in front of the window was a Christmas tree, its white lights twinkling among the silver bead garland and a multitude of ornaments. And beside it was her mother, smiling as she added another ornament.

Lacie's broken heart now felt as though it might explode.

"What…?" Tears welled in her eyes as they had only moments before. Except these were happy tears. She brought a hand to her mouth as if trying to keep everything inside. For the first time since Daddy died, there was a Christmas tree in the living room.

Mom came toward her then. "You were right, Lacie. I have been trying to get back at God. All these years, I've been angry." She slipped an arm around Kenzie's shoulder. "It made it hard to listen when my granddaughter so joyfully reminded me just how much Jesus loves me. Then I found this." She turned then and picked up a small box.

"What is it?" Lacie's bottom lip trembled as she watched her mother lift out a shimmering ornament that read Jesus Is the Reason for the Season.

"It was your father's last gift to me." Her mother's voice broke, her blue eyes shimmering with unshed tears. "I found it in the closet the other day, still wrapped, with a note that said Never Forget." She sniffed. "Kenzie was right. Jesus does love me. Enough to hear me out when I finally told Him how upset I was about losing your father."

Unable to hold her emotions in any longer, Lacie embraced her mother. "Oh, Mom. I know how much you miss Daddy." She sobbed.

"I do, sweetheart. More than you will ever know." She set Lacie away from her. "But I can't tell you what a burden has been lifted from me these last few days. My bitterness is gone. All because I finally said my piece."

"I'm so happy for you." She hugged her again. "I love you, Mom."

"I love you, too, sweetheart."

"Aunt Lacie." Kenzie tugged on her hand. "You need to come see this."

Swiping a finger across each cheek, Lacie allowed Kenzie to lead her to the tree, where she picked up a glittering Popsicle-stick snowflake ornament.

"My mommy maded this." Her dark eyes that were so like Matt's were alight with what could only be described as pure joy.

"She sure did." Lacie smiled at the memory. "And I got mad at her for using up all of the purple glitter." She laughed.

Kenzie giggled while Lacie continued to study the tree, which was filled with so many memories. The colorful palm tree ornament they'd gotten that year they vacationed in Florida. It had been her first time at the beach. The salt dough imprints of her and Marissa's hands when they were toddlers. And the Mod Podge photo of Lacie and her dad that she'd made in kindergarten.

She looked at the ceiling, blinking rapidly. So much joy. So much sorrow. *Thank You, Lord.*

Lowering her gaze, she noticed the stockings hanging from the bookshelf.

"My stocking." After grabbing a tissue from the table next to Mom's chair, she moved to the far end of the room to admire the handcrafted labor of love her grandma Collier had made for her before her first Christmas. Running a finger over the felt-and-sequin snowman, she smiled. How proud she'd been of her stocking, always eager to show her friends when they came over. Because no one had a stocking like hers. Except Marissa.

Just as it always had, her sister's teddy bear Santa stocking hung to the right of hers, the white felt cuff forever marked with a few chocolate smudges courtesy of an eight-year-old Marissa.

"I thought maybe Kenzie could use Marissa's stocking," said Mom. "For this year, anyway."

Recalling the three stockings hanging over Matt's fireplace, she sniffed. "I think that's a great idea."

Arms wrapped around her middle, she continued around the room, taking in all of the items that had lived in her memory, but hadn't seen the light of day in twelve years.

"Oh, Grandma Preston's nativity." Kneeling beside the side table, she felt as though she'd been transported back in time. How she used to love playing with the ceramic Mary, Joseph and baby Jesus. And while most adults would have objected, Grandma never took issue. Sometimes, she even joined in.

Standing, she saw her mother across the room, watching Kenzie, looking happier, more carefree, than she'd seen her in a long time. This was truly an answer to prayer. "I'm proud of you, Mom."

The woman hugged herself as she surveyed the space. "I'm kind of proud of me, too."

"Now we need some presents." Kenzie dropped to her knees in front of the tree, her small fingers moving from one ornament to the next.

Mom looked to Lacie. "That reminds me, how was your evening? Were you successful?"

Lacie's heart broke anew. While she and Matt had been successful in picking out gifts, the rest of the night had been a miserable flop. She didn't know what she was going to do. The Christmas they'd planned at Matt's, the one that had seemed so promising, probably wasn't even going to happen now. At least Mom had had a change of heart. Now Kenzie could wake up Christmas morning to a tree filled with presents and carols playing in the background, the same way Lacie had always done.

But what about Matt? What about the gifts they'd picked out? Would he still get Kenzie the sled?

"It was fine. Though we still have some decisions to make." The biggest one being whether she would stay in Ouray or head back east and away from Matt.

Matt came home from work the next day and dropped his gear at the door, only to spy the Christmas tree at one end of his living room and the bag of unwrapped gifts at the other. The sickening feeling that had plagued him all day intensified. He didn't know what to do now.

Shoving a hand through his hair, he collapsed onto the couch. He was a mess. These last few weeks his life had been fuller than he ever imagined and he didn't want that to change. Not now, not ever. Unfortunately, that's exactly what was about to happen.

All day long he'd tried and tried to make sense of it. He and Lacie had such a good time at the store. Everything had seemed fine. Yet she'd known. The entire time they were there, she'd known about the job offer and didn't say a thing. Why couldn't she have said something before they went to Montrose?

Because they still would have ended up in the same foul mood and that would have made it nearly impossible to think about shopping.

Glimpsing the stockings spread along the mantle, his heart ached. *J-O-Y.* That's exactly what Lacie and Kenzie had brought into his life. Without them he was miserable.

He dropped his head into his hands. *What do I do, God? What do I do?* Staring at the floor, he saw a sliver of white sticking out from beneath the couch. He picked it up, immediately recognizing the card with columbines on the front. It was a note his mother had written to him when she was dying. Something she'd done for each of her five sons. It must have fallen out of his scrapbook that day all those weeks ago when he'd first suspected he was Kenzie's father.

Opening the card, he again read his mother's words:

My precious Matt,
As the middle child, I know you often felt as though you didn't stand out, but you were always a shining light to me. A man of great character, with a stubborn edge,

you're kind and eager to help others. Traits some people might take advantage of, so guard your heart.

Tears blurred his vision and he looked away. "I wish you were here now, Mama."

He blinked a few times before allowing his gaze to drift back to her handwritten words.

Traits some people might take advantage of, so guard your heart. However, not so closely that you allow that something or someone special to slip away.

Lowering the card, he thought about Lacie. She was someone special all right.

And you're letting her slip away, doofus.

He shot to his feet. What was he thinking? He couldn't lose them. He had to find a way to convince Lacie to stay. And there was only one thing he could think of.

After a quick change of clothes, he hopped into his Jeep and drove the few blocks to the Collier house. Darkness had already fallen over the town when he pulled up, and while he'd often been to Lacie's at night, this time he found himself doing a double take to make sure he was at the right house.

There was a Christmas tree in the front window.

Deciding he was, indeed, at the correct house, he climbed out and started up the walk, past a dwindling pile of snow. He wasn't sure he'd ever been so nervous. *God, please let this work. I don't want them to go.*

He knocked on the door. A moment later, Lacie stood before him, looking as beautiful as ever in jeans and a sweater, her hair around her shoulders. Her expression unreadable, she simply stared at him through the storm door for the longest time, until he finally said, "Can I come in?"

She stepped back, allowing him entry.

"Matt!" Kenzie barreled toward him in her favorite bright pink outfit, arms outstretched. At least somebody was happy to see him.

He lifted her into his arms, savoring her sweet childlike aroma. "How's it going, small fry?"

"Come see." She was already trying to wiggle free.

He set her to the ground, only to have her hand take hold of his much larger one.

She tugged him into the living room. "We made Christmas!"

Turning, he took in the entire space. It was Christmas, all right. Everywhere he looked. There was even Christmas music playing in the background.

His gaze captured Lacie's before darting back to Kenzie. "Did you and Aunt Lacie do this?"

Kenzie stared up at him, her smile wide. "No. Grandma and me surpriseded her when she got home last night."

Grandma? Wait a minute. Barbara? But she— He looked at Lacie. "Your mom? Really?"

Arms crossed over her chest, she nodded. "I was pretty surprised myself."

He glanced around. "Is she still at the shop?"

"Yeah."

Just as well. He didn't need an audience.

"Look, Matt." Kenzie held up a small ceramic manger. "It's baby Jesus."

"I see that." He couldn't help wondering what had happened to change Barbara's mind.

Then he recalled Kenzie's determination to get home from church last Sunday and the way she adamantly shared the good news of Jesus with her grandmother. Could that have been what turned her around?

"Want to color with me?" His daughter was beside him again, peering up at him with those big brown eyes. "I gotted a Christmas coloring book." She held it up. "'Cept there aren't any horsies. Only reindeer."

Could the kid possibly get any cuter? No one could say no to that.

"Sure. Let's sit down at the table." Besides,

coloring was supposed to be relaxing. He could use a little of that as he gathered his courage.

While Lacie worked on dinner, Matt sat beside Kenzie, though it was difficult to stay focused with all the things he wanted to say to Lacie swimming through his head.

Nonetheless, he colored a reindeer on one page while Kenzie tended to the Christmas tree on the opposite page. Not near as easy as when they each had their own book to color. But since she had only one that was Christmas themed...

Elbow on the table, chin perched on her hand, his daughter let out a sigh. "I think I want to color by myself now."

"Are you sure?"

She nodded.

Standing, he ruffled her soft hair. "Okay, small fry. Let me know if you need my help." He sent her a wink before turning his attention to the kitchen.

Lacie was at the stove, stirring a pot of something that smelled really good. Any other time his stomach would have growled, but it was too tied in knots to do so now.

He took a deep breath. *Okay, Stephens, it's now or never.*

Pressing forward, he moved beyond the island to lean against the counter beside the stove.

"Smells good." Great, now she probably thought he was looking for a dinner invitation.

"Vegetable soup." She shrugged. "Not exactly a manly meal."

Time to cut to the chase, before he lost his nerve. "Lacie, I don't want you to go to Colorado Springs."

For a split second, he thought he saw a glimmer of hope in her pretty gray-blue eyes. "I know you think the best thing is for you to devote yourself to Kenzie, but she needs more." He lowered his voice. "She deserves two parents who love her. And, honestly, I can't go back to the way things used to be." Looking her straight in the eye, he took a deep breath and went on. "Marry me?"

Her expression went flat. "Very funny." She whisked past him and turned on the water at the sink.

"I'm serious, Lace." He followed her, not that he had that far to go. Smiling, he took hold of her now-wet hands. "I want us to be a family. Lacie Collier, will you marry me?"

Her gaze searched his for a moment and his hopes soared. Then her brow furrowed as she slowly shook her head.

She let go of his hands, wiping them against her jeans as she stepped away. "I—I'm sorry, but I can't do that."

He blinked, his heart feeling as though it had been ripped in two. He'd blown it. She wasn't interested in him.

What was he supposed to do now?

The only thing he could do.

He retreated. Moved to the table and placed a kiss atop his daughter's head, the first time he'd dared to show her that kind of affection. "See you later, small fry."

Turning to leave, he couldn't help noticing the beautifully decorated Christmas tree in the living room. The one at his house was every bit as nice, thanks to Lacie. But the tree at her mother's made one thing perfectly clear.

Lacie didn't need him anymore.

Chapter Seventeen

Matt sat behind the wheel of his sheriff's vehicle the next morning, feeling like a fool for leaving Lacie's with his tail between his legs instead of sticking around to ask her some questions he really needed answers to. Such as when was she leaving? What about Kenzie? When would he get to see her? And what about Christmas? Though it was obvious they'd now be celebrating at her mother's. But what about the gifts they'd bought for Kenzie? She was his daughter, after all, and he intended to spend Christmas with her.

Continuing along one of the county's back roads, he eyed the sleet/snow mixture that had been falling since shortly after sunup and racked his brain, trying to decide how to approach Lacie again. Not that his reasons weren't valid. It was just the situation was so…awkward.

His gaze shifted from the conifers lining the road to his right to the snow-covered mountains beyond the dormant rangeland on his left. He needed some advice and soon, otherwise he'd drive himself crazy. But from who? It wasn't like any of his brothers had ever been in a situation like this, or his father. Still, Dad seemed to be the logical choice. Especially since he knew more about Matt and Lacie's relationship than anyone.

By the time he bumped up the ranch's drive around lunchtime, the wintry mixture had turned to all snow. He parked between Noah's pickup and his father's dually, exited his Tahoe and hurried onto the deck. Good thing his father always had a pot of coffee on. Between the cold and lack of sleep, Matt could really use a cup.

He paused at the door, though. It had been a long time since he'd dropped by the ranch unannounced. Or even wanted to. Should he have called first?

No. Dad had shown him nothing but love and acceptance since that day he came to him. So Matt was going to let bygones be bygones.

Opening the door to the mudroom, two things captured his attention: the aroma of pine and the smell of coffee.

"Dad?"

"In the kitchen," the old man responded.

Matt kicked out of his work boots, thinking about that day he, Lacie and Kenzie had come out here to cut down the trees. The day Kenzie got lost. Or so they thought. That was the day he began to think of the three of them as a unit. A family.

Boy, had he been wrong.

Inside the kitchen, Dad sat at the long wooden table, eating his lunch. "There's some roast beef." He pointed toward the counter. "Help yourself if you're hungry."

"No, thanks." He started toward the cupboard. "I'll just take some coffee." He poured a cup, then joined his father.

Dad's dark eyes narrowed. "What's the problem?"

Matt sent him a curious look. He hadn't even said anything yet. "Who said there was a problem?"

"You did. Those lines in your forehead don't show up unless something's got you bothered. So what is it?"

He wrapped his cold fingers around the hot mug. "Lacie's been offered a job in Colorado Springs."

The old man frowned. "Surely she's not going to take it."

"Unfortunately—" he leaned back in his chair

"—I'm afraid she is." If she hadn't already. "But there's more to it than that."

His father picked up a potato chip and waited.

"I'm in love with her, Dad."

Shaking his head, the old man popped the chip into his mouth. "I hate to say I told you so—"

"Then don't. Please." He straightened. "I feel bad enough as it is."

"I'm sorry, son."

Matt stared at the black liquid. "It's just... I thought our relationship had moved beyond friendship."

Sliding his plate out of the way, Dad crossed his arms on the table and leaned closer. "I assume you told her you loved her?"

"I was going to, then she told me about the job offer. Even had the nerve to ask me how I'd feel about her taking it." He puffed out a disbelieving laugh. "I mean, you'd think she would have known."

"So what did you say?"

He let go a sigh. "I told her to do what she wanted to do."

Dad's face contorted. "Son, why would you—"

Matt shot to his feet. "I was angry, all right?" Gripping the counter, he stared out the window. "But I knew I'd made a mistake, so I went to see her last night." Over his shoulder, he looked at his father. "And I asked her to marry me."

Dad's brows lifted. "Well now…" He picked up his plate and moved beside Matt to set it in the sink.

"Yeah, it was kind of spur-of-the-moment, but I was contemplating it even before she said she was leaving."

Inches apart, Dad narrowed his dark gaze. "What did she say?"

"She said no."

"What on—" The old man threw his hands in the air. "Did you tell her you wanted her to stay?"

"Yes."

"Did you tell her you loved her? That it wasn't just about Kenzie? That you wanted to spend your life with her?"

Matt scrubbed a hand over his face. "No, I did not." How could he have been so stupid?

Suddenly still, Dad looked appalled. "You didn't?"

"Apparently, I overlooked some very important points in my speech, okay?"

Hands on his hips, his father glared at him. "Matt, you're my son and I love you. But from one stubborn man to another, you're about to blow this. You need to get yourself over there right now and tell Lacie how you feel about *her*."

He pondered the old man's advice. "You're right, that is what I need to do." Pushing away from the counter, he grabbed his mug and set it near the sink before heading for the door. "I just hope she'll listen to me."

Dad followed him into the mudroom. "Matt, if Lacie is worth having, then she's worth fighting for. You just need to make sure she understands that your feelings for her have nothing to do with Kenzie. You got it."

He shoved into his boots. "Got it." Straightening, he held out his hand. "Thanks, Dad."

The old man took hold and reeled him in for a hug. "I'll be praying for you, son."

"Thanks." He was almost out the door when his radio went off. He listened close.

Shoplifting suspect. Older-model Ford Explorer, dark green. Last seen heading north on 550 out of Ouray.

Right where he was.

"Gotta go, Dad." He radioed dispatch as he closed the door, threw himself into his Tahoe and took off down the drive. Unfortunately, his talk with Lacie was going to have to wait.

The snow had picked up, making it difficult to see. Yet as he reached the end of the drive, a dark green Explorer whizzed past.

"I love it when things are easy." He turned on his siren and lights and took chase. His windshield wipers thumped back and forth across the glass as he bore down on the vehicle in question a half a mile later. But the driver wasn't having any of it. He accelerated, weaving around the vehicle in front of him.

What few cars there were moved out of the way, allowing Matt to follow. The suspect pressed on. Swerved, but regained control.

"Come on, buddy." Matt picked up speed. "Pull over."

They continued through the neighboring town of Ridgway, past the reservoir.

Finally, Matt closed in again.

The fellow veered left.

What was he—

Ice.

The Tahoe went into a spin. Matt took his foot off the gas pedal and tried to regain control. Everything was a blur. Then he saw it. Another truck coming toward him.

Matt did the only thing he could do. He braced for impact.

While the snow continued to fall outside, Lacie hung a shirt on one of the circular racks at The Paisley Elk with a little too much force, causing a portion of the display atop the rack to topple. How blind could she have been? Matt was interested only in Kenzie, not her. Why else would he have proposed a loveless marriage?

Well, loveless for him anyway. Still, she couldn't live that way, hoping, wondering, if someday he might fall in love with her.

But who could blame him? Kenzie was not only his daughter, but adorable in every way. Just look at the way she'd shared her five-year-old faith with her grandmother. And Mom had responded in a way even Lacie couldn't have imagined.

Listening to the Christmas music that her mother was now playing at the store, she righted the black velvet jewelry forms and repositioned their beaded necklaces. As soon as Christmas was over, she needed to leave Ouray. Even though the company in Colorado Springs had given her a week to make her decision, she may as well go ahead and accept their offer. Sure, it would mean being away from Mom again, and there'd be a challenging few months while she and Kenzie adjusted to a new town, new school and new job, but they'd be okay.

At least, she hoped so.

Yet as she returned to the storage room at the back of the store, the sadness and unease lingered. *Help me, God.*

She was about to grab a couple more dresses when her phone vibrated in her back pocket.

Pulling it out, she immediately recognized the number on the screen. Her heart raced with anticipation.

A glance over her shoulder revealed an empty shop, so she decided to take the call.

"Lacie, this is Jim Duncan with Bridal Veil Builders in Telluride."

"Yes, sir." Nervously tucking her hair behind her ear, she paced back into the main area of the shop. Why was she so anxious all of a sudden?

"My partner and I have talked things over and we'd like to offer you the job," said Jim. "We were quite impressed with your designs and think that you would be a great addition to our team."

Yes! She mentally thrust a fist into the air.

Of the two positions she'd interviewed for, this was the one that interested her the most. Not only because of the location, but because it was a custom builder, not a big corporate builder, giving her a chance to spread her wings as a designer and try some new things.

But within seconds, her excitement fell flat. Hadn't she just decided it would be best to take the job back east? To get away from Ouray and Matt? "Um, that's great. Really. Thank you."

"You sound hesitant."

She perched on the arm of the black leather love seat near the dressing room, indecision gnawing at her gut. "I've received another offer. And while I haven't accepted it yet..." Though if it wasn't for Matt...not to mention her heart...

"I understand." Jim's voice remained even. Undeterred. "Why don't you take the weekend to think things over, then?" His generosity made her smile.

"Thank you so much." Relief flooded through her, though she was sure it was only temporary. "I promise, I'll be in touch with you first thing Monday morning."

"Looking forward to it. Have a good weekend, Lacie."

Standing, she ended the call, wanting to cry and do a happy dance at the same time.

A job in Telluride was the best of both worlds. Aside from a great position, she could stay in Ouray, where she'd have friends and family to help her with Kenzie. But now that she knew how Matt really felt, she wasn't sure she wanted to. Her heart would break every time she saw him.

But a move to Colorado Springs would mean Kenzie would almost never see Matt. And she didn't want to do that to either of them.

So what was she supposed to do?

She rubbed her forehead. This was going to be a very long weekend.

The door jangled and she looked up to see her

mother rushing toward her with Kenzie in tow. And while Kenzie appeared fine, Mom looked distressed.

Lacie approached the front of the shop, watching as her mother settled Kenzie at the table with the dollhouse. "What is it?"

Mom patted her granddaughter on the back. "You stay here, sweetie, while I talk to Aunt Lacie." The woman was practically winded by the time she reached her. She took hold of Lacie's arm, tugging her toward the scarf display at the back of the store.

She couldn't imagine what had her mother so riled up. She sent her a curious look. "Are you okay?"

"Clint called." Mom sucked in a breath, her blue eyes boring into Lacie. "There was a car accident. I don't have many details, just that Matt was unconscious when the ambulance took him to the hospital."

Her throat tightened. She blinked. Several times. *God, please let him be okay. Please!*

Mom put an arm around her shoulders and aimed her toward the door. "I'll stay here while you go on to Montrose—"

Lacie stopped in her tracks. "What for?"

Her mother shot her a disbelieving look. "To the hospital so you can be with Matt."

Lacie felt as though her heart was shattering

into a million pieces. If anything happened to Matt... What about Kenzie? She didn't even know he was her father.

She turned away, wrapping her arms around herself, not wanting her mother to see the pain that threatened to swallow her. "It's not my place."

"Not your place?" Taking hold of Lacie's elbows, an incredulous Mom stepped in front of her.

Through tears and the occasional sob, she told her mother everything that had transpired between her and Matt in the last few days. "I love him. But I can't marry someone who doesn't love me."

"Oh, sweetie." Mom hugged her tight. "You are so misguided."

"What do you mean?" She took a step back and stared at her mother.

"Young lady, you told me the truth when I needed to hear it, so now I'm going to give you some of the same. Matt loves you."

"He loves Kenzie." She sniffed. "And that's okay. I get it."

"Lacie, do you not see the way that man looks at you? The way he lights up whenever you walk into the room?"

"Then why didn't he tell me?" She swiped a finger over each cheek. "I mean, who asks someone to marry them without telling them you love them?"

"Matt Stephens." Mom's head bobbed with each word.

Lacie frowned, too afraid to buy into her mother's observations for fear she'd only be let down again.

"He's a man, Lacie. Sometimes they assume things." Mom crossed her arms. "Your father didn't tell me he loved me very often, but I still knew."

"Yeah, but I bet he told you when he proposed."

Seemingly frustrated, her mother continued to watch her, pinched expression and all. "Okay, Miss Know-It-All, does Matt know how you feel about him?"

Though she'd never said anything, he must have had some clue. Why else would he have thought she'd agree to marry him? "I—I guess so. I mean, it's not like I came out and told him."

"Oh, my dear, sweet daughter." Mom wrapped her arms around Lacie's shoulders. "If Matt doesn't survive this accident, you might never get the chance."

Chapter Eighteen

Matt didn't have to open his eyes to know that his entire family was in the room.

"Why is he asleep?" said Andrew. "I thought people with concussions were supposed to stay awake."

"Sleeping actually helps the brain heal." Noah had been on the rodeo circuit long enough to know. "It's a loss of consciousness they're more concerned about."

"All I know is that he got T-boned pretty good," said Jude. "When I came up on that scene, I wasn't sure he'd even be alive."

"God is good." Dad sounded kind of choked up. "Guess He knows Matt and I have some lost time to make up for."

"I'm just waiting for him to open his eyes and tell all of you to shut up." Did his baby brother,

Daniel, know him or what? Because that's exactly what he was about to do.

Except his head was killing him. Not to mention the entire left side of his body. And that incessant beeping noise wasn't helping. *Somebody shut that thing off.*

"Would one of you boys tell someone to get in here and change his IV bag?" The old man was getting annoyed. "That noise is about to drive me up a wall."

"I got it," said Jude.

Things grew quiet then. Except for that stupid beeping.

"Let me get this taken care of for you." A woman's voice. A nurse maybe?

Whatever the case, the beeping had stopped. *Thank You, Lord.*

"Look who I found out in the hall," said Jude.

Who was it? Matt tried to open his eyes, but the lights were so bright.

"I was hoping you'd come," said Dad.

Who? Who was he hoping would come?

"How is he doing?" Lacie?

"Much better than they first thought." Dad cleared his throat.

"Good." *It was Lacie!* He could tell by the fragrance of her perfume. Like wildflowers in July.

Now if he could only… He struggled to open his eyes, but those lights…

"Would you like us to leave you alone?" asked Dad.

"Oh, that won't be—"

He might not be able to open his eyes, but he could still talk. "*Yes… Please…*"

"Matt?" He felt his father's calloused hand cover his.

"Would somebody kill the lights?" His request, or rather, demand, was followed by the shuffling of boots against linoleum. He could envision his brothers hurrying to do his beckoning. Of course, that would be a first.

"Daniel, close them blinds." A moment later, his father continued. "Okay, Matt. It's as dark as we can possibly get it."

For the first time since they'd moved him to a private room, he opened his eyes ever so slightly. Enough light from the hallway shone in for him to recognize the standard features—bed rails, TV hanging just below the ceiling, big, round wall clock, uncomfortable-looking chair.

With the head of his bed already elevated, he searched the concerned faces gathered around him until he found Lacie. Man, she was beautiful.

He blinked a couple of times, becoming more alert. "Would you guys mind if I talked to Lacie alone for a few?"

Dad held up a hand. "Whatever you want,

Matt." Turning, he nodded toward the door. "Come on, boys. You heard him."

He watched them leave then shifted his attention to a seemingly nervous Lacie. "Where's Kenzie?"

"With my mom."

He figured as much. "Come here." He held out his right hand. To his surprise, she took hold. Despite the throbbing in his head, he tried to smile. "Boy, are you a sight for sore eyes."

Her pretty gray-blue eyes studied him, the corners of her mouth tipping upward. Did she have any idea how much he loved her?

No, she didn't, because he'd never told her.

He caressed her hand with his thumb. "Why are you here?"

Lifting a shoulder, she said, "They said you were hurt."

"Not as badly as they first thought." His gaze briefly traversed the sterile room before returning to her. "Concussion, broken arm, a few bumps and bruises...nothing life threatening."

"I didn't know that, though. And I couldn't..." Pressing her lips tightly together, she looked away.

"Could I get you to put this railing down—" he bumped it with his elbow "—so you can sit beside me?"

Nodding, she did just that, carefully adjusting

the IV tubes that extended from his arm before easing onto the side of the bed.

He again took hold of her hand, urging her closer.

Finally, she looked at him, her eyes shimmering. "I couldn't let you die without telling you how I felt."

His heart dared to hope. He moved his hand to her cheek. "Well, I'm not dying, but I'd still like to hear it."

She drew in a deep breath, a tear slipping onto her pretty face, but he brushed it away with his thumb. "I love you."

"Funny, that's—" He cocked his head, the movement making him wince.

"Are you okay?" Her eyes were wide now.

"Yeah." Lowering his hand, he closed his eyes until the pain subsided. "Remind me not to make any sudden movements."

"I'm sorry." She caressed his arm.

Finally, he opened his eyes. "As I was about to say—" his gaze found hers "—that's exactly what I wanted to tell you, before I had to chase that shoplifter."

She laughed ever so softly.

"I messed up, Lace. I mean, sure I'd like Kenzie to stay here in Ouray, but there are plenty of law enforcement jobs near Colorado Springs. If you choose to go, I'll simply have to follow you."

He threaded his fingers into her hair. "But I really wish you'd choose to stay here with me. Not because of Kenzie, but because you're the best thing that's ever happened to me. I love *you*, Lacie Collier, and I want to spend the rest of my life showing you just how much."

Her tears fell in earnest now as he tugged her close and kissed her with everything he had. Which may not be much right now, but if she'd agree to be his, he'd do everything he could to correct that.

When they finally parted, he rested his forehead against hers. "So what do you say, Lace? Will you marry me?"

A teasing smile played across her pretty lips as she placed a hand on his chest and leaned back. "On one condition."

He was in a hospital bed and she wanted conditions?

He lifted a brow. "And that is…?"

"We can be married by Christmas. Assuming you're well enough, that is."

Now, that was a provision he could live with. He'd marry her right now if he could, but—"You know Christmas is only eight days away. I thought weddings usually took months to plan."

"That's for big weddings." She shrugged, adjusting his white blanket. "I prefer something smaller. More intimate. Say, with just family."

Things were looking up. "I think we can make that happen."

"Good." She smiled, but didn't say anything else. Did she know how to make him crazy or what?

He tugged her toward him again. "I'm still waiting for an answer, Lace."

"Looks like I'll be taking that job in Telluride, after all."

"You got it?"

She nodded. "They called this afternoon." Her expression turned serious then, her hand softly touching his chin. "I would love nothing more than to be your wife and grow old with you, Matt. So yes, I will most definitely marry you." She touched her lips to his. "I love you, Matt."

"I love you, too, Lace. Now and always." He brushed a hand over her hair. "Now, why don't you go get my family? Because we've got a wedding to plan."

Lacie made her way through the darkened house in her bare feet Christmas morning, pausing to plug in the lights on the tree and quietly turn on some Christmas tunes before continuing into the kitchen to get the coffee going. This Christmas hadn't turned out at all like she'd expected. Only a month ago, she'd feared she and Kenzie would have no Christmas at all. And now—

One strong arm found its way around her waist. "Merry Christmas, Mrs. Stephens." Matt's whispered words were a caress on her ear.

She turned into his embrace, though his other arm was still in a cast and would be for several more weeks. "Merry Christmas to you, Mr. Stephens." Placing her hands on his broad shoulders, she pushed up on her toes and kissed her husband with no hesitation, and no doubt of his love for her.

They'd married last night, in a quiet ceremony at Granger House, with Mom, Kenzie and all of Matt's family in attendance. There in front of Carly's Victorian Christmas tree, with the snow falling outside and only tiny white lights and candles illuminating the parlor, she and Matt had pledged their love to one another forever. Things couldn't have been more perfect. Then they all celebrated with more food than eleven people could possibly eat. Her new sister-in-law had pulled out all the stops for them.

"I take it Kenzie's not up?" Matt kept his voice low.

"Not yet." Lacie and her mother had taken a couple of days to overhaul one of the bedrooms at Matt's for Kenzie. They'd painted, hung curtains and bought new bedding, giving the little girl the pony room of her dreams.

Of course, they should have known better than to show it to her earlier in the week, because she'd been a little miffed that she'd had to wait until last night to sleep in it.

Lacie grabbed two mugs from the cupboard as the machine finished brewing. Once Matt was well, they'd need to make a run to Denver to get all of her things out of storage.

"Hey, Lace."

"Yeah." She eyed her husband, who was now standing by the back door.

"Come look at this."

Still holding the cups, she moved beside him, gasping when she looked outside. "It must have snowed all night." The two blue spruces in the backyard bowed under the weight.

"And it's still coming down," he said.

"In that case—" she returned to the coffee-pot "—shall we snuggle on the couch while we wait?"

"Mmm, I like the way you think." He gave her another kiss.

"How are you feeling this morning?" Cup in hand, she carefully nestled beside him a few minutes later and took a sip of the hot liquid.

"Well, I just married the woman of my dreams, I'm about to spend my very first Christmas with my daughter and I now have someone to make my coffee for me every morning. I'd say things are pretty good."

She playfully swatted his good arm. "Ha! You just *think* I'm going to make coffee every morning." Setting her cup next to his on the appropriately named coffee table, she twisted to face him. "Seriously, how's the arm? The hip? The leg?" While his head seemed to be fine, he still walked with a slight limp.

"A little better every day."

"Good, but I don't want you overdoing it today." At least they had only one house to go to instead of three. Carly had graciously offered to host everyone at their place so Matt wouldn't have to do so much traveling. And probably so they could help eat all those leftovers. Though if she knew Carly, she'd have a new round of food going today.

"But what about Kenzie's sled?" He motioned a hand toward the window. "I mean, with all this fresh snow…"

Her mouth fell open. "Don't you dare even think—"

He silenced her with another kiss.

Wrapping her arms around his neck, she deepened the kiss, weaving her fingers into his short hair.

"It's Christmas!"

She jumped at Kenzie's excited announcement and pulled herself off the sofa with Matt in tow.

"Merry Christmas, sweetie." She smoothed a hand over her robe. Being a newlywed as well as a parent was going to take some getting used to. She peered up at a blushing Matt. But they'd find some way to balance it all out.

"Hey, small fry." Matt kissed Kenzie's cheek as he scooped her up into his good arm. "Merry Christmas."

"Merry Christmas." Kenzie sleepily brushed the hair away from her face, all the while eyeing the tree surrounded with presents. She'd been so great this week, wanting to help take care of Matt and taking extra care not to bump or hurt him in any way. Of course, her favorite thing had been writing her name on his cast.

"You don't suppose there's anything under that tree for you, do you, small fry?"

Kenzie nodded, her smile no longer sleepy.

"What do you say we check it out, then?" Matt set her to the floor and the three of them inched closer.

"Oh, those stockings look much fatter than they did last night." Lacie retrieved Kenzie's, pausing just long enough to admire the diamond wedding band that now adorned her left hand.

She passed the stocking to Kenzie before grabbing hers and Matt's. "Let's see what's in it."

Kenzie sat cross-legged on the floor and shoved her hand inside. "I gotted some new crayons." She reached in again and pulled out a small board book. She studied the cover. "A baby Jesus book."

Matt leaned toward Lacie. "That is one smart kid. She figured that out just by looking at the cover."

She winked at him. "We'll chalk it up to good genes."

"What is that?" Kenzie crawled to her feet, her dark eyes wide as she looked at the tree.

"Whatcha see there, Kenz?" Matt stood beside her.

"This!" She ran to the tree and pointed to the sled that was leaning against the wall.

"Do you know what that is?" asked Lacie.

"Uh-huh." She bobbed her head. "It's for the snow."

"It sure is." Matt's grin had him looking like a kid himself. "What do you say we take it up to the sledding hill later today and you and Lacie can try it out?"

"But don't you want to ride it, too, Matt?"

"I do, but I can't until I'm healed."

"Oh, yeah." She frowned.

"But we've still got a lot more winter ahead

of us. So as soon as I'm better, we'll make a day of it, okay?"

"Okay."

It wasn't long before all of the presents had been opened and the living room was littered with the wrapping. So while Matt rested on the couch, Lacie went to the kitchen to heat up the sausage-and-egg breakfast muffins Carly had sent home with them last night. When she returned to the living room, Kenzie was beside him and he was reading her the baby Jesus book that had been in her stocking. He finished the story right about the time Lacie set the platter of muffins and some napkins on the coffee table.

"Matt, are you my daddy now?"

Lacie froze. To have Kenzie call him Daddy would be a dream come true for Matt, even if Kenzie didn't know the truth yet.

"'Cause I never had a daddy before," Kenzie continued.

Matt looked at Lacie, his eyes wide with anticipation. "Well, I guess now that Lacie and I are married and we'll all be living in the same house..." He was trying hard not to insinuate himself.

Lacie sat down beside her niece. "Kenzie, do you want Matt to be your daddy?"

"Uh-huh."

She glanced at her husband, who was blinking heartily. "Why don't you ask him, then?"

Still leaning against Matt's right side, Kenzie peered up at him with eyes just like his. "Matt, will you be my daddy?"

He seemed to have a hard time finding his voice. "Small fry, I would love nothing more than to be your daddy."

Kenzie grinned. "Aunt Lacie, Matt said he'd be my daddy."

"I heard." And she couldn't be happier for both of them.

Kenzie jerked her head back to Matt. "Thank you, Daddy." She giggled, then hugged him before hopping down to play with her new toys.

Lacie watched the man she loved with all of her heart. She'd never seem him so dumbfounded. But then she knew how he'd longed to hear Kenzie call him Daddy.

She took hold of his hand and curled beside him. "I'd say this was a pretty good Christmas, huh?"

"Are you kidding? I've gotten everything I ever could have wanted and more." He wrapped his arm around her. "God has brought me two of the greatest blessings ever. You and Kenzie." He kissed her forehead. "It's a dream come true."

Sitting there in the warmth of his embrace, watching the snow fall outside, with Christmas music playing in the background while Kenzie danced in front of the tree, she realized that her dream had come true, too. She'd wanted Kenzie's Christmas to be extra special, like the kind Lacie'd had when she was a kid. They'd gotten exactly that, plus a husband and a daddy, too.

Kenzie moved in front of them, wearing her new pink cowboy boots and hat with her pajamas. "This is the bestest Christmas ever!"

With more joy in her heart than she'd ever imagined possible, Lacie hugged her niece. "I'd have to agree with you, Kenzie." The three of them were a family. And that was the best gift ever.

* * * * *

If you enjoyed
THE DEPUTY'S HOLIDAY FAMILY,
be sure to check out
these other wonderful tales
by author Mindy Obenhaus:

THEIR RANCH REUNION
THE DOCTOR'S FAMILY REUNION
RESCUING THE TEXAN'S HEART
A FATHER'S SECOND CHANCE

Available now from Love Inspired!

Find more great reads at
www.LoveInspired.com

Dear Reader,

I have wanted to write a Christmas story set in Ouray for a very long time. Probably because it combines two of my favorite things—Christmas and Ouray.

There's something extra special about the Christmas season that makes us want to believe that anything is possible. Then again, it is Jesus's birthday. And with Him, all things really are possible.

Nothing is too big for God. Not our mistakes or our sins. Because of Jesus, we have been redeemed. That means God can forgive us, change us and even use what we would consider our biggest regrets for His glory, if we simply trust in Him.

When I first began this story, I knew Matt was a true hero. That despite an error in judgment and a rocky relationship with his father, he was a man of integrity who didn't hesitate to help someone in need, whether they were a strange woman being taken advantage of by an inebriated guy or an independent elderly teacher suddenly unable to take care of herself.

And then we have Lacie, a woman who gave up everything for her niece—her job, her home and her dreams of finding love. But God had other plans.

These two giving people were perfect for each other. And I hope you enjoyed watching them fall in love as much as I did.

I'm looking forward to introducing you to the remaining Stephens brothers and spending some more time at Abundant Blessings Ranch. Until then, though, I'd love to hear from you. You can contact me via my website, mindyobenhaus.com, or you can snail mail me c/o Love Inspired Books, 195 Broadway, 24th Floor, New York, NY 10007.

See you next time,
Mindy

Get 2 Free Books,
Plus 2 Free Gifts—
just for trying the Reader Service!

LIS17R2